The
Blind Spot

*Also available in Perennial Library
by John Creasey:*

The Blind Spot

John Creasey

Harper & Row, Publishers, New York
Cambridge, Philadelphia, San Francisco, Washington
London, Mexico City, São Paulo, Singapore, Sydney

A hardcover edition of this book was originally published in England under the title *Inspector West at Bay*. A hardcover edition of *The Blind Spot* was published in the United States in 1954 by Harper & Brothers.

THE BLIND SPOT. All rights reserved. Printed in the United States of America. For information address Harper & Row, Publishers, Inc., 10 East 53rd Street, New York, N.Y. 10022. Published simultaneously in Canada by Fitzhenry & Whiteside Limited, Toronto.

First PERENNIAL LIBRARY edition published 1987.

Library of Congress Cataloging-in-Publication Data

Creasey, John.
  The blind spot.

  Originally published under the title: Inspector West at bay.
  I. Title.
PR6005.R517I48   1987   823'.912   87-45202
ISBN 0-06-080895-0 (pbk.)

87 88 89 90 91 OPM 10 9 8 7 6 5 4 3 2 1

The
Blind Spot

1

Acid

Chief Inspector Roger West of Scotland Yard took off his hat to mop his forehead, and as his hand-kerchief dabbed he felt a stinging pain on the back of his right hand. One moment he was sticky hot, like the dozens of people in Fleet Street near him; the next his hand seemed to be on fire, spots burned on his cheeks and chin, and the pain stung his eyes to tears and made him catch his breath.

He dropped the handkerchief.

A girl, passing him, screamed out in agony and clapped her hands to her face. Men just ahead swung round at the sound. West, blinded by the tears, saw nothing. He felt a hand on his left arm, and said between his teeth: "I'm burning."

He clenched his teeth, and his lips curled back in the effort not to groan; and he could hear the girl screaming in his ear. Confused voices sounded above the noise of the passing traffic, a newsboy's cries, the sound of footsteps. His hand seemed to be bubbling as if molten fire were on it; so did the spots on his face.

He heard a gruff voice, "Now, what's all this?"

That was a policeman.

The gruff voice and shrill ones alternated with the screaming, which sank to a low moaning. People hurled advice, others cried out, and a phrase kept being repeated:

"Look at his hand."

"Look at her face."

"Look at his hand."

"Look at—"

West hardly knew how he stopped himself from groaning, for the pain grew worse. Someone touched his hand, and it felt as if his whole body caught fire. Then, people touched him more gently, and soon he was leaning against a shop window. He fought against panic; and the pain grew no worse. He opened his eyes and could see blurred figures, including several policemen. He heard the mutter of voices, the words: "Doctor," "ambulance," "they're hurt," and then another word which stuck in his mind and held his thoughts in a vice.

"Vitriol."

That was it; someone had thrown vitriol and caught his hand; vitriol or other acid. It was eating into his flesh now. He'd seen people scarred by acid burns often enough, now he knew what it felt like. It was as if all the pain in the world were going through his hand and arm.

A policeman with a pasty face stood just in front of him.

"You'll be all right, sir, come with me."

"Wash it—" began Roger.

"Yes, sir, just along here."

Roger was led into a milk bar and his hand was

2

thrust under the cold-water tap, while the constable splashed water from a jug onto his face. He felt relief at once as the acid was washed away.

"Now we'll bathe it with this, sir."

The constable had been busy.

"Alkali?" asked Roger.

"Solution of washing soda, sir."

"Weak?"

"As weak as it should be." The constable sounded as if he knew the drill.

He bathed Roger's hand and face, then suddenly backed a pace.

"Are—you Mr. *West?*" his voice shrilled.

"Yes." The pain was receding. "Did anyone see who threw it?"

"The sergeant's inquiring, sir."

"The—girl?" asked Roger; he hadn't had all the pain in the world.

"Fainted," said the policeman. "She'll be all right, they've taken her to a café. Your face isn't bad, sir, only the back of your hand, you needn't worry." He spoke in an aside as another man came up. "It's Handsome *West.*"

It sounded as if he were uttering the name of an oracle.

A deeper voice came. "Sorry to worry you, sir, but did you see anyone?"

Roger made himself think back. A youth with a pale face, walking toward him; a middle-aged man, almost alongside the youth. A boy on a bicycle, coming practically straight at him, because he'd been very near the curb. A well-dressed woman, whom he'd seen out of the corner of his eye. The small shops, the hanging signs, and the crowds in Fleet Street; he'd seen all that, and knew

3

that three people had been close enough to throw the acid.

The youth with the pale face; the middle-aged man; and the boy on the bicycle.

He managed to say: "Boy on bike. Short, pasty-faced boy, walking. Man about fifty, black coat, gray trousers, Homburg."

Then he heard the shrill ringing of an ambulance bell; they hadn't lost much time.

Janet West heard the telephone bell ring in the sitting room of her Bell Street house, and thought nothing of it. Life of late had been tranquil—much more tranquil than the wife of a senior officer at Scotland Yard should expect. She was in the kitchen, greasing small cake tins. It was just after four on an April afternoon, the sun shone as fiercely as in mid-summer, she wore a flowered cotton frock, her dark hair was slightly damp at the forehead, and her face needed powdering. She wiped her hands as the bell rang again, and as she went along the hall of the small, detached house, she heard voices: boys' voices. She smiled, and caught a glimpse of her two sons, the massive Scoopy and the lean but wiry Richard, talking to Jonathan, a neighbor's child. They were in earnest consultation, and Scoopy looked baking hot.

Janet lifted the telephone.

"Janet West here."

"Just a moment, Mrs. West," said a girl. "Sir Guy Chatworth would like a word with you."

It was as if the sun had been blotted out and icy winds swept from arctic wastes. Janet actually shivered. Chatworth was the Assistant Commissioner at Scotland Yard, and didn't make social

4

calls in the middle of the afternoon. She felt her knees go weak, and dropped into a chair: Roger's chair. This was about Roger and almost certainly meant bad news; otherwise, why should Chatworth ring up?

"Mummy!" That was Richard, gaily. "Can I have a sweet?" A pause, and an afterthought came hastily, "Please."

She didn't answer.

"Mummy!" Richard ran past the open door toward the kitchen; Scoopy and Jonathan continued their talk outside. "Mummy!" called Richard in a most insistent voice and with an edge of disappointment. "Where are you?"

She called, "Yes, have a sweet, and go out to play."

"Can Scoopy have one, too?"

"Yes."

Why on earth was Chatworth so long coming through?

"Can Jonathan?" asked Richard, appearing at the door and looking at her with a pair of startlingly blue eyes, large and fringed with long, curling lashes. "And could—"

"Take a sweet to everyone outside and go and play!"

"Yes, Mummy," said Richard, startled into demureness. He went off, and began to sing.

The telephone line buzzed and crackled, and then the girl spoke again: "I'm sorry to keep you waiting, Sir Guy—"

"Who's that?"

Janet recognized Chatworth's voice.

"You're through, sir."

5

"About time," growled Chatworth. "Hallo—Mrs. West?"

"Yes." The only indication of her fear was Janet's voice; it was too loud. "Is that you, Sir Guy?"

"Yes, Janet." He was softening her for the bad news. "Now don't get worried, I haven't come through to tell you that Roger's at death's door or anything like that. He's had an accident, but there's no danger at all."

Janet said, "*Oh*. What—" She broke off, feeling faint.

"He's burned his right hand rather badly, and is at St. Giles's Hospital. Nothing to worry about. He won't be home tonight, safer for them to keep him under observation, but you can go along and see him if you like. Not before seven. I've made all the arrangements, you won't have any difficulty getting in."

"Thank—thank you," said Janet huskily.

"Have you living-in help? Sitters-in?" Chatworth was a gruff martinet most of the time, yet surprisingly human. "I'll send someone, if—"

"No, I can manage," said Janet, and wiped her hot, damp forehead. "How did it happen?"

"Some lunatic threw some acid—it caught a girl rather badly. Roger seems to have been in the way. It's nothing to worry about, you understand."

"I see," said Janet, and shivered again. "Did they mean—"

"Aimed at the girl, almost certainly," said Chatworth. "Got her, too—she'll lose the sight of one eye, and might be totally blind. It was just bad luck for Roger, if you can call a week or two's sick leave bad luck."

"Week or two? *Month* or two!"

6

Chatworth chuckled. "I can tell you're feeling better. Seriously, you needn't worry. He had some pain, but the doctors have put that right. It'll leave a scar, of course, but nothing much—I've been into all that. There was a constable handy, and he did a good job, washed off most of the stuff before it could do its worst. How are those two children? One's a godchild of mine, don't forget, although why I let your husband talk me into—"

"They're fine," said Janet. "Fine. Thank you for telling me. Good—good-by."

"'By," said Chatworth.

Janet put down the receiver and slid into the chair, leaned back, and closed her eyes. The cold-ness had gone, she began to feel too hot, and had several ugly visions. Of Roger, and someone throwing acid at him; of Roger in agony. Of what would have happened if a lot of the beastly stuff had struck his face. She couldn't shut the visions out, even when she stood up and went along to make tea.

They had a daily woman, whose afternoon off always coincided with emergencies. As today. The children needed tea. It would be better to have something to do than sit about, but she feared her-self at times like this; she lost her self-control too easily, flared up at the boys. The shock was greater because it had come out of the blue; it was months since Roger had been involved in a violent case.

Sick leave—

It would do him good, might even be a blessing in disguise; that was how he would look at it, any-how. She found herself smiling as she put on the kettle. The boys were unusually quiet. She filled the cake tins and put them into the oven, then

7

checked the heat; it was too hot. Well, they would be eatable, anyhow.

The telephone bell rang again.

She caught her breath as she went slowly to the sitting room; she would hate the sound of that bell for a long time to come. She lifted the receiver.

"Janet? It's Norah here," said Jonathan's mother. "Will it be all right if Scoopy and Richard stay to tea? Jonathan's persuaded me that it's time they did."

"Oh, wonderful!"

"Eh?" Norah Thomas sounded puzzled by that heartfelt cry.

"Sorry," said Janet. "I mean—Norah, keep them for a bit, will you, and pop in when you can? Roger's had an accident. Nothing serious here, but—"

"Oh, you poor dear! I'll come at once, Doris can give them their tea."

Norah rang off.

The kettle was boiling, and Janet made tea, then realized that she had a headache, heavy and throbbing, across her eyes. It was just after half-past four. It would take half an hour to get to the hospital, near Covent Garden market, so she had plenty of time. She took the tea into the sitting room, and was lighting a cigarette when Norah came in, tall, slim, dark-haired, anxious.

Janet told the story.

"My dear, how beastly. Now you mustn't worry about tonight, I can come in and look after the boys when they've finished tea, and I'll put them to bed. Just don't worry a bit."

Janet found tears in her eyes.

She took extra care with dressing and with her make-up, and ordered a taxi for half-past six; she would be at the hospital on the stroke of seven. It was too hot to travel by bus, anyhow. The boys were shrieking in the next-door garden. It was six o'clock when she was ready, and she wished she hadn't started to change so soon. How was Roger? Had Chatworth minimized the injuries? Acid burns were devilish. There was the girl, too, disfigured for life, possibly blinded.

A ring at the front door broke across the thoughts.

She went to the head of the stairs from the front bedroom, with its double bed and the furniture of dark oak, which was beginning to look slightly shabby, and peered down. She could see the open door and the letter on the mat; no one appeared to be there. She went down. The sealed, typewritten envelope was addressed to Roger. She had trained herself not to open his letters, because he often received urgent notes from the Yard. This one puzzled her. If it had been sent from the Yard, the messenger would have made sure someone took it in. She turned the envelope over; it was a thick, cream-laid one of good quality. If it were urgent, the Yard ought to be told.

She went back into the kitchen and cut the envelope open with a knife. There was a single sheet of cream-laid paper folded inside, and in the middle, neatly typed, a single sentence:

This is only the beginning.

2

Mark Lessing

The taxi pulled up outside the hospital, and Janet climbed out, paid the driver, and walked briskly up the steps. The letter was in her handbag. She'd done nothing about it yet; she couldn't think what to do. Whenever she let her thoughts run, she was caught up with terror—what could it mean, except that the acid had been meant for Roger, not the girl?

She ought to have telephoned Chatworth, at once; she ought to telephone him from here. She looked at the receptionist at the desk, who was talking to a porter.

"Good evening."

"I think my husband is here," said Janet. "I'm Mrs. West, and—"

"Oh, yes, Mrs. West," said the receptionist, a blonde with a husky voice and plenty of glistening lipstick. "We were told you would be coming about seven, the porter will take you up to the ward."

"Thank you."

"This way, ma'am." The porter was gray-haired

and round-shouldered, with a lined, careworn face. "Still hot, isn't it? We'll pay for this, mark my words, we always have a bad summer when it sets in like this in April."

"Yes, don't we?"

The porter kept on talking. They went up a flight of stone steps, then along a passage with a rubber flooring which muffled footsteps. Red and green lights showed at the corners and over some of the doors; these were the private wards. A nurse came out of a room, and the patient inside laughed. A doctor came out of another, frowning. Roger's? The porter went to the end room along a wider passage, and a card on the door said: *Do not enter.*

"It'll be the doctor," explained the porter. "Just doing the rounds. Won't be two minutes."

He was too optimistic, they waited ten before the doctor came out, a youthful man; too young, Janet thought fearfully, to be in charge of Roger.

The doctor was fair-haired and Scottish.

"Are you Mrs. West?" His accent was pleasing, his blue eyes friendly and reassuring. "He's expecting you, but don't stay too long. I've given him a sedative, and after a good night's sleep he'll feel fine."

"You're sure?"

"Positive, don't be worrying."

Roger was leaning back on his pillows in a small, green-painted room. His face was pale, and had a few small adhesive-plaster patches on it. His right arm was outside the clothes, and bandages from just below the wrist covered the whole hand. He raised his other arm an inch, and smiled, but his eyes told her how much pain he'd had.

11

"Hallo, my sweet." His voice was husky. "Sorry about this. Did they scare you?"

She went across and kissed his forehead.

"No, Chatworth was very good."

"The old man himself, eh."

"So I should think." Janet pulled up a chair and sat at the side of the bed. "Is it—very painful?"

"Not now. Forget it. Light me a cigarette, will you?"

She lit a cigarette and saw the relish with which he drew at it. Now that she was here there was so little to say. He wasn't badly hurt, she could tell; but it wouldn't be just a passing injury, and had been quite bad enough. His eyes were glassy; she'd seen him like this at times when he had been on duty without sleep for two, even three days. She'd had plenty to say then about working himself to death.

"Boys know?" asked Roger.

"No, not yet. Norah's looking after them. I thought I'd tell them in the morning. She's told them that I had to come and meet you."

"Neighbors are a help," said Roger prosily, and had spirit enough to jeer at himself. "Hark at me! I'm not so sorry for myself as for the girl. If I ever find that swine, I'll—"

He broke off.

Janet tightened her grip on her handbag, and said: "Never mind what you'll do to him, darling, just worry about getting better."

"Yes, ma'am. Seriously, though, see if there's anything you can do to help the girl, will you? Parents, and that kind of thing." Would he never stop thinking about others? Must he always put himself

12

last? "I've told Bill Sloan everything I can, but short of meeting the people face to face—"

He broke off, and yawned.

"Did I tell you what Richard said at breakfast?" Janet asked in a gentle voice. "We were all at the table, and ..."

Five minutes later she stopped talking; for Roger was asleep. She crept out of the room, looked back at him from the doorway, then closed the door and stared down at her white linen handbag. Inside was the letter. She had actually wondered if she would be able to bring herself to tell him. She could call herself the complete fool. She hurried toward the stairs, missed her way, then caught her breath.

Anyone could get in here, find Roger's room—

This is only the beginning.

She found the stairs, went down them blindly, reached the hall, and smiled mechanically at the porter and the receptionist. It was dark, and much cooler; she had a summer coat, and was glad of it. As she reached the bottom step, she saw a man step out of a car. No one else was about, and the gateway was some way off. She flinched, but the man called out eagerly:

"Jan?"

"Mark!"

"Hallo," the man said, drawing nearer. "Did I scare you? Sorry. How is he?"

"Not—not too bad. Mark, how did you know?"

"It's in all the evening papers," said Mark Lessing. "I've been out of town all day, bought a paper half an hour ago, called the Yard and learned that Roger was here. No hope of seeing him, I suppose?"

13

"He's asleep. Mark, can you spare this evening?"

"As long as you like."

"Take me to see that girl's people, and then home?" asked Janet.

"Of course. Do you know where the girl lives?"

"No—they'll tell us at the Yard."

"We might as well look in," Mark said.

They went toward his car, a Jaguar which shone dull green in the light of the hospital. A man in white stood with his back to a window, a nurse came hurrying across the car park. Mark Lessing opened the door of the car, and Janet got in. Mark was the one man above all others she could talk to—Roger's closest friend. She sat back, as he steered the car into the narrow street which led to Covent Garden, then turned toward the Strand. Here the bright lights showed the windows of the closed shops, the interminable stream of traffic and people. Mark turned right, toward Trafalgar Square, passed Nelson's floodlit Column, and turned into Whitehall. Large gray buildings loomed up.

Chelsea lay to the southwest, near the Thames. Mark drove smoothly, and they passed Parliament Street and the little turning which led to Scotland Yard. As they approached Parliament Square, with the lighted face of Big Ben looking down at them, Janet said: "Stop, Mark. Somewhere. I want to talk."

"We'll stop on the Embankment." Mark turned left, then left again, and pulled up near the Yard, opposite the river, in the light of the lamps which spanned Westminster Bridge. "What's the trouble?" he asked, too casually.

14

"I hardly know what I'm doing. The police think it was an accident, meant for someone else, but—"

"Now, come!"

"Look," said Janet, and fumbled at her bag, opened it and pushed the envelope at him. "Don't finger it too much," she added hastily, "it might have fingerprints."

She watched him as he held the note by the edges and unfolded it. He was handsome in a severe, even an aloof way; brown-haired with a rather sallow complexion, fine brown eyes, a pointed chin, and well-shaped but thin lips; a man she could trust absolutely. His hair waved a little —not so much as Roger's. It wasn't fair, like Roger's, either; yet she seemed to see Roger sitting there, instead of Mark.

"Well, well," said Mark, when she had told him how the note had been delivered. "And you haven't shown this to Chatworth? Or Bill Sloan?"

"No, I—I had some foolish idea of waiting until I'd seen Roger. Mark, it does mean what I think it means, doesn't it?"

"It could." Mark forced a smile. "It might be about something quite different, I shouldn't take everything for granted. Feel like tackling them in here?"

He pointed to the wall and the big white building of the Criminal Investigation Department beyond it; several windows glowed with light, and a constable stood on duty at the gates.

"Not really," said Janet. "Will you tell them?"

"Yes. Let's drive in," said Mark.

The constable held them up, recognized Janet, and let them pass. Other cars were already parked in the wide yard. Janet sat where she was, Mark

15

hurried to the steps and disappeared, moving very quickly; he was tall, and his movements had an athlete's grace. He didn't look round.

He had not questioned the grim significance of the note.

As a friend of Roger West's and the author of several slim books on criminology which made even experts applaud, Mark Lessing was *persona grata* at Scotland Yard—unless he deserted theory and took up practical detection, when Chatworth stopped being affable. A bareheaded sergeant in the hall greeted him cheerfully, said what a shame it was about Mr. West, and told him that Mr. Sloan was inside somewhere, he'd come in half an hour ago.

"Try the canteen first, sir, if I was you."

"Thanks."

Mark went through into a white, cement-walled passage, but didn't try the canteen. He went upstairs to the floor where Roger and most of the Detective Inspectors worked. He tapped on a door, was told to enter, opened it, and saw two men sitting at a desk, with a pile of photographs in front of them, and a pile of records on a trolley by their side. Both were big men; fair; florid. At first sight they might be taken for brothers. There was no true facial resemblance, and Sloan, the one facing Mark, was the larger.

He stood up.

"Hallo, Mark. Can't say I'm surprised to see you."

"Hallo, Bill." They shook hands. "He's not doing so badly, I'm told."

"Badly enough," Sloan growled. "You know Detective Sergeant Peel, don't you?"

The other man stood up; he was younger than Sloan by several years, and had a more eager expression; his eyes were bright and clear.

"Oh, yes, we're old friends. Working overtime?"

"Roger told us what two or three of the people nearby looked like. We're checking through the known vitriol throwers, just in case we strike lucky. Haven't done, yet." Sloan motioned to the pile of photographs. "We've a call out for anyone who saw it, and there'll be a crowd in the morning. Funny thing is, it doesn't seem to have been anyone to do with the girl. That's as far as we can find out. Her parents have been here, and her fiancé. She hadn't a care in the world, no jilted boy friends, none of the things we can usually trace when they start this business." Sloan ran a hand over his close-cropped hair. "It may have been meant for someone else nearby, of course, and that'll lead us a pretty dance. Anyone who knows it was meant for them probably won't come forward."

"Pity," said Mark. He offered cigarettes; Peel preferred his pipe. "What do you make of this? It was delivered to Bell Street this evening. Handle it carefully," he added, as Sloan grabbed. "There might be prints."

"What's this?" Sloan frowned.

"Read."

Sloan read, and barked, "When did this come?"

"About six, delivered by hand. The caller didn't wait to see Janet, just rang the bell and threw this into the hall. You can imagine what she feels like."

Sloan said, "Can I! Where is she?"

"Outside, in my car."

"The boys?"

"At home, with a neighbor. They—"

Sloan swung round, lifted the telephone and barked, "B2 Division, and hurry." He held the receiver and looked at Mark, but didn't speak. Peel went round to his side and read the note. "Chelsea?" Sloan asked into the telephone. "Sloan of the Yard here. Will you detail a couple of men to keep a special watch on West's house?...The children are there, his wife isn't.... Yes, a neighbor's looking after them.... I don't know, I'm just being careful." He paused. "Thanks a lot," he finished, and put the receiver down.

"So you feel like that about it, too," said Mark.

"If they'll do that to him, they'll do anything," Sloan said. "Let's get that letter checked for prints."

3

No Prints

Sloan and Lessing walked up to the next floor, past closed doors where lights showed at the bottom and sides. A few men passed, and most of them recognized Lessing. As they approached the little room where articles were examined for fingerprints, a burly man approached and grinned.

"Getting some good advice at last, Bill?"

"That's right," said Sloan.

"How's Roger?"

"Doing nicely."

"These acid throwers are just about the worst of the bunch," said the burly man, and passed on.

Sloan opened the door of Fingerprints. There was a bench beneath a window, and above it were two powerful electric lights. One corner of the bench was piled high with a motley collection of articles: cigarette cases, bottles, knives, an automatic—a glorified junk heap. Another, larger heap was in a corner on the floor. Between these piles stood a thin-faced man in his shirt sleeves, sinewy forearms bare, a pair of thick-lensed glasses perched on the end of his nose. In his right hand, he held a camel-hair brush which might have come out of a children's painting set, and he was brushing a gray powder over a soiled white handbag. He didn't look round until he had finished with this.

"Busy, Percy?" asked Sloan.

"Who, me?" Percy turned, to show hollow cheeks and a bony chin. "No, I'm never busy. That little lot wants doing tonight, if you please. It'll take about seven days with two of us working, and I'm here on my own until midnight. But I'm not *busy*." He sniffed. "All I have to do is brush gray powder over the damned things and blow it away. Easy. I can do it in my sleep. What do you want?"

"Try this for me, will you?" Sloan held out the letter and the envelope.

"No favoritism, it'll have to take its turn." Percy looked at Mark, without recognizing him. "I'll fit it in before twelve, if—"

"It's the West job."

"Oh, is it?" Percy sniffed and looked sour and took the envelope by the edges. "I suppose you've dabbed your mitts all over it, and half a dozen people have handled it, so by the time we've sorted it out it'll look like a specimen from the monkey house."

He carried it to the light and peered at it closely, turned it this way and that, sniffed again and then began to brush gray power over it; a tin of the powder lay open on the bench.

"Funny," he said.

"What's funny?"

"Nothing much on the surface, where you'd think they'd handle it. A few woman's prints here

20

and there. I can see men's prints at the edges—two different lots," he added. "The paper wasn't fingered much when it was put in the typewriter, though." He breathed hard through his nostrils, and went on, "Nor was the envelope. Gloves, I fancy."

"I'll be back in a minute," Sloan said. "Coming, Mark? Oh, I forgot—this is Percy Law, our master of fingerprints. Mark Lessing, a friend of Roger's."

Law blinked behind his glasses.

"So you're Lessing, are you?" he said. "Read a little book of yours the other day. Last week. *Hypnotism and Crime*. Not half as bad as I thought it would be."

Mark grinned. "Thanks."

He went out with Sloan, to Records, which was on the same floor. A big man with a pale face was on duty at a table near the door. The room was rather like that of a public library, but instead of books round the shelves there were folders. A card-index system was in several cabinets, by the side of the desk.

The pale-faced man looked up.

" 'Lo, Bill. Evening, Mr. Lessing."

"Sam, let me have Mrs. West's prints, Mr. Lessing's and mine, will you?"

Sam gave a slow smile. "Been up to no good?"

"You'd never believe it."

"Oh, wouldn't I?" said Sam dryly. He opened one of the cabinet drawers, stifled a yawn, left them and came back in two minutes, carrying three foolscap sheets of paper. Each had a name, an address, general particulars, and fingerprints in ten spaces, each space marked with words, such as *"Right Index Finger. Right Thumb."* The prints were

21

black and showed up very clearly. "In the special section," he said, "but it would go hard with you if you ever did anything you shouldn't, Mr. Lessing!"

"He never does," said Sloan. "Thanks."

Back with Percy Law, they compared the prints on the sheet with those that Percy had found on the paper and envelope; Janet's were spread wider than Mark's, whose prints showed only at the edges; there was only a trace of Sloan's.

"That's the lot," said Law. "Whoever typed that wore gloves or had adhesive tape over his fingers. Can't help you. What's it all about?"

"That's what we're finding out," said Sloan.

On the way back to his own office he was frowning and silent. Inside, Peel was standing up, and all the photographs were now turned down on their faces—he had finished with them. He looked hopefully at Sloan.

"Anything?"

"No prints, the chap who typed that note didn't mean to be identified that way."

"Chap?" asked Peel.

"Oh, it could be a woman."

"When typing's the clue, *cherchez la femme*," said Peel. "You know, Bill, this could be ugly. If that note means what it seems to mean, someone threw that stuff at Roger, and he was lucky to get away with it. It also means they'll try again. Does Mrs. West know?"

"She guesses," Mark told him.

"I suppose she would."

"We'd better not do anything to scare her too much," Sloan said. "It's a pity we can't talk it over with Roger right away. He might know of someone who's got a grudge."

22

"There are about three hundred and seventy people who might. Three hundred of them are inside." Peel frowned and rubbed his chin. "We'd better go through all the files and find out who Roger's picked up and sent down. If this is a grudge, it will probably be from someone who's had a long stretch and come out lately. I'll get started on it."

"You go home and get some sleep," said Sloan. "You haven't been off duty since midnight last night. I'll have someone else looking through the records of the people Roger's sent down, and we'll go through them together in the morning."

"Okay," said Peel.

"And before anyone tells Roger about this, I'll have a word with Chatworth," Sloan went on. "Everything will be all right at the hospital if we have a man outside the ward. It'll be all right at Chelsea, too. Going to stay the night at Bell Street, Mark?"

"Not unless Janet asks me to. If I offer she'll realize that we're worried."

"I'll leave that to you, but the Division will have a man back and front." Sloan lit a cigarette and puffed smoke toward the ceiling. "Could be a scare, of course."

"Meaning?" asked Mark.

Sloan said thoughtfully, "The evening papers all carried the story. Anyone could have read it. Someone who had a grudge against Roger might have decided it was a good way to scare the wits out of him and his wife. We can't assume that the writer of that note did the vitriol job—yet."

"Ten to one he did," said Peel.

Sloan shook his head.

"I wouldn't take evens. I wouldn't like to go to

23

Chatworth with half a story, either." He turned to Mark. "You'd better go down to Janet. If there's anything else we can do, let us know."

"Right," said Mark. "Thanks. Oh, where does that girl live?"

Janet was sitting in the car and staring toward the Embankment. Farther along, lights showed at the windows of the big buildings behind the plane trees in the gardens. There was less traffic now. Mark took the wheel, and slid off toward Charing Cross Station.

"What did they say?" Janet asked tautly.

"That it might be someone who read about it in the evening papers, and had a foul idea. They're checking everything, and they certainly won't go to sleep on it."

"So they're taking it seriously."

"Of course. How are things fixed at home? Like to have some dinner first, then see that girl's people, if you really mean to?"

"Roger asked me to."

"'Nuff said," said Mark. "Perhaps we'll go there first."

The injured girl lived in Lambeth, just over the river. Her elderly parents were badly shocked; they seemed vaguely grateful for the visit, and pathetically anxious.

Mark and Janet left after half an hour, and had dinner at a small restaurant in Soho, where Mark was regarded as a favored customer, and where the cooking was superb and the wine admirable. Mark didn't hurry. Janet seemed glad to be able to sit back, look round the small, old-fashioned room, watch the other diners and the waiters, who seemed to be falling over each other in anxiety to serve. She didn't suggest that Mark should stay the night at Bell Street either then or when he pulled up outside the house, just before ten o'clock.

A light was on in the front room.

"Will you come in for a drink?"

"Thanks, yes."

Norah Thomas was listening to the radio, which was tuned into a French station with the volume down low. They had a drink. Norah went off at half-past ten. Mark lit a cigarette as he sat back in Roger's chair. Janet's color was better than it had been earlier in the evening, and her eyes were brighter.

Yet he wasn't easy in his mind when he left just after eleven.

A constable was walking slowly along Bell Street. He passed the small two-storied houses with their neat little gardens, showing up clearly in the light from the windows. He saluted Mark, who said good night and felt rather easier as he drove toward the Embankment and his bachelor flat in Victoria, small, beautifully appointed. He had three hobbies—criminology, old china, and music; and he wasn't thinking about music or china as he put his car in a nearby garage and walked the hundred yards to his flat in Candor Street.

Here the streets were narrow and the houses tall. It was a long road, at the back of Victoria Street and near Westminster Cathedral. Street lamps were glowing, no one was about; there were shadows in the doorways. Mark scowled as he unlocked the front door of the house; his flat was on the fourth and top floor. The stairs were carpeted. No lights showed, and he switched on a landing light from the hall and went upstairs. He couldn't get his mind off the horror of the fact that someone had thrown vitriol at Roger West. He began to blame himself for not having stayed with Janet; what would she be feeling?

He unlocked the door of his flat, switched on the light, and closed the door. He did everything with great deliberation, because he wasn't really thinking of what he was doing. By now he knew that he was already on edge; this had done something to him that he hadn't experienced for a long time; his nerves were at a stretch. Just a single sheet of note paper with a single line of typing on it—and it could do this to him. He knew better than to try to laugh it off.

He opened the door of his living room, and stepped in—and stood still, hands raised.

On top of a grand piano which filled a corner of the room were some books; his own books. There were five; and the leather binding had been ripped off each and the pages torn in half. They were left neatly, the torn pages by the side of the beautifully tooled leather.

The shock quivered through him.

These were first editions; prize copies, signed by many of the experts whose help he'd obtained when preparing them. The binding was both costly and hard to get. In the book shelves on either side of the fireplace were hundreds of other books, not his own work; valuable first editions, beautifully printed modern books; but none of these was touched. Whoever had done this thing had selected his prize five, from a top shelf.

He went forward, stretched out to pick one up, and drew his hand away sharply. It was *Hypnotism and Crime*. There might be fingerprints on it. He swung round and snatched up the telephone from a table near his armchair in the corner. He dialed Whitehall 1212, and asked for Sloan.

Sloan hadn't left.

He listened. . . .

"I'll come right over," he said. "Don't touch anything."

Mark put the receiver down, scowled at the torn books, and began to feel less irritable. It wasn't an irreparable loss, but it was bad enough; just sheer vandalism. Someone had broken in here, could have done untold damage and, instead, had selected just those five books; as if in warning.

Mark went into the bedroom.

Nothing seemed to have been touched since the maid—it was a service flat—had turned down the bed. Certainly nothing was damaged, yet one thing caught his eye. A thick, cream-laid envelope lay on his pillow, with his name typed on it: Mark Lessing, Esquire. He hesitated before picking it up, took out a handkerchief, slit the envelope with a penknife, but knew what to expect before he unfolded the single sheet of cream-laid paper.

The message read:

This is only a beginning.

4

Chatworth

Sloan took a whisky and soda which Mark poured out for him, said, "Cheers," and sipped. He was sitting in an easychair, opposite Mark's; he had been there for an hour, and two of the men who had come with him had just left. A third was downstairs.

It was after midnight.

"Not a sign of a print, on the books, on the doors, anywhere," Sloan said. "No one in the other flats noticed anything. Not a damned thing! But I wish to blazes he hadn't started on you, there's no knowing where he might stop."

Mark shrugged.

"It should give us a lead."

"Meaning, if it's revenge he's after, it was a job you helped on."

"Isn't it obvious?"

"Could be," said Sloan. "Most people know when you've been working with Roger. It's less than a dozen cases, all told. I shouldn't take it for granted you had anything to do with making this gent start hating—if he's as clever as he seems to be, he'll spread the net to you simply to suggest that you were involved in the case when he was sent down. It's that much too obvious."

Mark said, "Maybe."

"Oh, we'll follow the line." Sloan sipped. He was thinking hard, and just keeping the conversation going. "Must follow every line, after all. We'd be making a mistake if we assumed that it was someone Roger's sent down. It could be another grudge. It could even be that he's started on a job and someone is trying to scare him off. Roger has a habit of starting jobs early, before they really come under the Yard's jurisdiction. We'll have to tell him everything pretty soon."

Sloan closed his eyes, and after a minute's silence spoke almost casually.

"No ideas yourself, have you?"

"Don't be an ass."

"Sorry." Sloan opened his eyes and grinned, finished his whisky and soda, and stood up. "Feel safe on your own?"

"Why not?"

"Meaning that he's done all he wants to do tonight," mused Sloan. "You're probably right, but don't forget that he's good. He picked that lock downstairs and the one on your front door, as if he's been doing it all his life. One of the neatest jobs I've seen—he had a skeleton key, of course. It might be a help—we know most men who can do a job like that. I'm sorry about those books, though, it must be a blow."

"Roger's was harder."

Sloan shrugged, and went to the door. Mark saw him out of the flat, came back, and instead of going to an easychair sat at the piano. He didn't put the top back, but began to play softly, a soothing tune; after a while he lost himself in this. His dark hair began to fall over his forehead, he kept brushing a lock out of his eyes. The look of strain on his face faded slowly. He did not play loudly— there would be too many protests from his neighbors; but the music banished thought of crime and devilry. He played for half an hour, then sat back, smiled at the keys, and went to bed.

He was up just after seven.

At eight he telephoned the Yard.

Roger had passed a comfortable night, and there had been no alarms at Bell Street.

Sloan, brisk and fresh at ten o'clock that morning, smoothed down his hair, collected the memos which he had already prepared, and left his office. None of the other five Detective Inspectors who shared it had put in an appearance; two were out on a case. He had spent an hour with eye-witnesses of the attack in Fleet Street, and had plenty of fresh evidence that only one person in twenty could boast good powers of observation. All had seen Roger and the girl after the scream; only two thought they had noticed anything that might help.

It was an event for Sloan to go and see the Assistant Commissioner; schoolboy-headmaster relationship came to life again. Chatworth was sound, but his moods were unpredictable. The one man at the Yard who really seemed able to handle him at all times and in all circumstances was Roger West. When Roger was in circulation Sloan seldom saw the A.C. alone.

His office was on the second floor.

Sloan tapped.

"Come in," called Chatworth, and sounded affable.

He was a big, burly man, running to fat. His large round face was reddish brown; he spent every minute he could in the country, walked a great deal, could hold his own at most sports. He had grizzled hair, with a bald patch which was as brown as his face, clear blue-gray eyes, and bushy eyebrows. He wore a light-brown tweed suit, which helped to make him appear bigger than he was, and looked like a farmer who had been dragged from his fields and placed in a modern jail. Some quirk in his temperament made him like his office sleek and streamlined. In a weak moment the Office of Works had allowed him to have glass-topped desk, tubular steel furniture, and a black carpet. He looked as out of place as a farm worker in a Mayfair drawing room.

He didn't smile. "Oh, it's you. Come and sit down."

"Good morning, sir."

"What's all this about West?"

"It's not good," began Sloan. "It—"

"Now listen, Sloan," said Chatworth with an ominous rumble. "West gets vitriol thrown at him and seems lucky not to have been blinded. The reports say that he had his hand in front of his face, and that saved him. I don't need telling it's not good."

"Sorry," Sloan said, his heart sinking.

"Tell me exactly what you've done and what you think."

Sloan sat erect on his chair, and made his report as if he were in the witness box at Bow Street.

31

Chatworth kept nodding and grunting, but didn't actually interrupt. Sloan kept nothing back; Chatworth had a knack of forcing issues if he thought anything was being withheld.

Obviously he hadn't heard of the vandalism at Lessing's flat, and his eyes rounded when Sloan reached that.

Sloan finished.

Chatworth pushed a black box across his glass-topped desk, and said: "Have a cigarette."

"Thank you, sir."

Chatworth lit a small black cheroot; the smell was abominable.

"Now, what have we really got?" said Chatworth. "A man or woman with a grudge, two type-written notes, no fingerprints. A man who can pick a lock with anyone. No one saw him at Lessing's flat, I take it."

"We've questioned everyone—there isn't a clue."

"Hmm. I see your point about Lessing being dragged in to make a red herring. Could be. On the other hand, Lessing has been pretty useful to West on several big cases. Better go through the records and get the names of everyone who—"

"I've done that."

"Oh. Good. Any line to follow?"

"Three people might be worth looking up," said Sloan. "Jacob Kennedy came out six months ago. He'd been sent down for ten years and got full remission. Blackmail, black market, and currency frauds, and he was always a nasty piece of work. He let himself go in the dock and swore he'd get square with West. He's in London, and must have had plenty of money tucked away, he's living like a millionaire. Then there's Doc Gorley—the big drugs case. He also had ten years, but twice attacked a warder at Dartmoor, so he didn't get much remission. He's out, living in the East End with a drab he knew before he went inside. I wouldn't trust Doc far. The third is Paul Wiseman, who went down for seven years. Company frauds. He was very much the gentleman, but at his arrest he put a bullet through one of our men and won a reputation for violence. All three of them might have nursed a grudge over the years. Each has the type of mind to try to do something like this."

"What are you doing?" Chatworth asked pointedly.

"Peel's started inquiries with them all."

"Yes, Peel's the right man for this job. You'll be in charge, of course, until West is about again. Told West about the notes?"

"No."

"Think we should?"

"I think we'll have to," said Sloan. "He might know something we don't. He's tough enough to take it. His chief worry will be his wife and the boys, and if we make sure they're all right that worry will be over. He certainly won't pine because he might be on the spot. I want him to see some photographs of people who've thrown vitriol, anyhow—he was betting on a pale-faced youth who was walking toward him, and we've three who might fit. Shall I tell him the whole story when I go to the hospital?"

"Check with the doctor first."

"I'll do that all right," promised Sloan.

*   *   *

The hospital authorities said there was no reason why Roger shouldn't be told.

Roger sat up in bed and looked through the morning newspapers. His hand was not really painful, but was numb and stiff. The spots on his cheeks burned a little, but not enough to worry about. The long night's sleep had steadied his nerve, he felt well enough, was annoyed that he had to stay here. He had expected a caller from the Yard earlier—it was now after eleven o'clock—and he also expected Janet. He was in a mood to be peevish, when the door opened and Sloan came in.

" 'Morning, Roger!" Sloan was breezy.

"Oversleep?" growled Roger.

Sloan grinned, glanced at the patches on Roger's cheek, pulled up a chair, and sat down.

"You don't expect me to change my habits because you're having a rest cure, do you? They tell me you're doing pretty well."

"As soon as I can get off this bed I'll—"

"You take it easy," said Sloan. "You'll have plenty to do when you come out, and you'll want your wits about you. Had any crazy thoughts while you've been brooding?"

"Only about vitriol throwers."

"Any idea who might have his knife into you?"

Sloan, still breezy, saw the change of expression which came over Roger's face, and guessed that the thought was completely new.

It was, and hit Roger hard. He studied Sloan's face carefully, told himself that Sloan wouldn't joke, that he really meant it. The possibility that the acid had been meant for him struck an ugly

34

note. He shifted his position, and his expression was set, strained.

"Let's have it."

Sloan didn't mince words or try to evade any issue. He told him of the precautions they'd taken with Janet and what had happened at Mark Lessing's flat.

None of this seemed real to Roger. It was some time before his mind really started to work on it; he relaxed, settled down on his pillows, and let his thoughts run. Sloan finished, took out cigarettes, and then started to put them away again.

"I'll have one, thanks," said Roger. They lit up. "Jacob Kennedy—Doc Gorley—Wiseman. Yes, if it's a revenge job, any one of them might be behind it. Mark was in all three cases—he used to do much more with me than he does now. I'm not forgetting the possibility that the smack at Mark was a red herring, either. What's Chatworth say?"

"He takes it all very seriously."

"He would." Roger drew hard at his cigarette. "Any hope of identifying that boy?"

"I've the photographs here," said Sloan, and drew a large envelope out from inside his coat. "There are five—all vitriol throwers, they've all been inside. They're not so young—the youngest is twenty-three. That fit with your youth?"

"It could," said Roger, and held out his left hand. "What about the middle-aged man and the boy on the tradesman's bike?"

"In the clear, I think. We've about fifteen people who saw the incident waiting at the Yard now. I want to get back and have another word with the ones whose statements are interesting. Two have said they thought that the youth walking toward

35

you threw something, but each describes the youth differently. One says he was fair, the other dark."

"Between colors," Roger said. He found it awkward to open the envelope, but Sloan didn't help him. "The chief worry is Janet. I think it might be a good idea to send her away, with the boys."

"If she'll go."

"She will, if it really looks serious," said Roger. He glanced at the first photograph and put it aside. "She won't take any risks with the boys, and I can't see her being separated from them. She won't be satisfied with what we've done so far, of course." He glanced at the second photograph and put that aside too, then looked straight into Sloan's eyes. "Could it be a hoax?"

"I shouldn't like to bet on it."

"I suppose not."

Roger glanced down at the third photograph— and started. Sloan moved forward swiftly.

"That him?"

"That's the boy," said Roger softly. "He was coming toward me, I couldn't forget him if I tried. Now we're on the move."

5

Bertie

Roger glanced up at the door, Sloan looked round, and Mark Lessing appeared—smiling, sporting a red-carnation buttonhole and carrying gloves and stick.

"And I've been feeling sorry for you," he said. "I ought to have realized you'd be plotting dark deeds. 'Morning, Bill."

Roger said, "Nice timing, Mark. Pull up that other chair. How's Janet?"

"I've just looked in at Bell Street. She had a good night, and looks it. Richard's thrown a slight asthma attack, and she couldn't get along first thing, but she'll be coming soon after lunch."

"Slight?" Roger asked quickly.

"Oh, yes. I've seen the little beggar, and he's nearly over it. Pity about that asthma, but he seems to be growing out of it." Mark sat down. "Done any brilliant detecting?"

"I think we've caught the little swine," said Sloan. "That is, he's identified." He tossed the picture to Mark. "Bertram Downs, known as Bertie, aged twenty-three. At the age of eighteen went down for four years for throwing vitriol over a girl friend who didn't want him for a boy friend any more. He's been out for some time and kept quiet since, but Roger recognized him in Fleet Street."

"I wouldn't mind a word with Bertie myself," said Mark.

"You keep out of this." Roger touched his hand. "If one of the crooks you helped me to send down is on a mission of vengeance, the quieter you keep the better for your health."

"Not my point of view at all," Mark demurred.

"Try to get the right angle," said Roger dryly.

Sloan stood up. "I'll go and get things moving; the quicker we pick up Bertie Downs the better. Ever had anything to do with him yourself?"

"No," answered Roger.

"So he hasn't a personal motive," said Sloan. "I'll look in or send a man as soon as we've got him. Keep your fingers crossed, we may have the big shot by tonight."

"And we may not," said Roger.

Sloan shrugged and went out. Mark thrust his hands in his pockets and leaned back uncomfortably on the upright chair. The only things he and Roger had in common, in appearance, were good looks.

Friendship lasting over twenty years had brought them very close together.

Mark broke the silence. "Any ideas?"

"Jacob Kennedy, Doc Gorley, or Wiseman," said Roger, half smiling.

"I've been thinking over possibles and reached the same trio. They're all as bad as they come, and they're good haters. But one thing makes each unlikely," Mark went on. "None is a fool. Only a fool would start a vendetta against a Yard man."

"One of them might have a blind spot." Roger shifted his position. "While things are quiet, keep an eye on Janet, won't you? And soften her up for the possibility of taking the boys away. They break up next week for the Easter holidays, so there's nothing to stop it."

"Except Janet," Mark observed. "She'll go if you go. You'll probably have to, anyhow."

"Not on your life," said Roger. He groped for his cigarettes, and Mark lit one for him. "Anyhow, when Sloan's had a chat with Bertie, we might know a lot we don't know now." He picked up the photograph. Bertie Downs's face was uninspiring; he had smallish eyes and rather a full mouth—Roger knew it in the flesh as a pasty moon of a face. "He certainly didn't think this up himself," he said. "I hope he knows who he did the job for."

The world, his family, the police, his neighbors, even the people he didn't know and who passed him in the streets, were set against Bertie Downs. The world was his enemy; he hadn't a friend. He was so full of self-pity that no one who knew him had any time for him.

Bertie's first vitriol victim had recovered remarkably well, was married to Bertie's one-time rival, Jim Stubbs, and lived two streets away from Bertie. Occasionally he saw her. If he had a friend it was Doris Stubbs; she never passed him in the street without a word of greeting. She didn't trust him, of course; no one trusted him.

If he had been asked, Bertie would have said that the police hounded him. If he happened to be looking into a shop window, the police would hustle him along. If he happened to stop outside a private house, they would talk about loitering with intent to commit a felony. If he wanted a job, there was always the black guilt of his past to stop him from getting it. A youth without any imagination, he could not see life beyond the confines of the East End; and then only his little part of the East End.

It wasn't a good part.

He lived in Bethel Street, near the docks. There was still a small church at one corner. The church was the only building of any size at all. The rest were little better than hovels, built of brick in a long terrace which curved slightly into a crescent. The front doors opened straight onto the street; behind each was a tiny square of garden which backed onto the garden of the house behind. Some houses were filthy, some spick and span. Some gardens were filled with crops, in season; others were like garbage patches. Some curtains were in rags; others were washed and ironed and mended regularly.

Bertie lived at Number 67. This was halfway along the street, in the middle of the curve. Opposite was a lamppost; Bertie spent a lot of time supporting that lamppost. The curtains of Number 67 were filthy, and the stench which came when the front door was open had to be smelled to be believed. Wallpaper was hanging in strips from the walls, the bare floor boards were dirty. It was rented by an old crone, Ma Diggett, and she slept and lived in the kitchen and let the other five rooms for a pittance; each tenant "did" for himself.

Bertie's room was on the top floor.

He scratched a living by doing odd jobs—running messages, touting for shops, picking up what he could at the dog tracks. He had one suit which was almost in rags and another, for "best," which looked quite respectable. He shaved only once a week, for his beard was thin and silky, so usually his face looked dirty. His little eyes were a pale blue.

As he lived, he hated.

He hardly knew whom he hated—unless it was everyone. The Salvation Army girl who tried to help him, and on whom he could rely for a cup of tea or a sandwich; the Welfare Officer at the nearest police court, who occasionally found him a few days' work; the policemen who "hounded" him—he classed them all together. Anyone who had made a study of psychology would have agreed that Bertie had a hate complex; that he felt none of the usual warm emotions of gratitude; that he was an outcast, largely of his own making.

He was one of many like him in the squalid parts of the East End; worse than most, but not the worst of all. He lived from hand to mouth, and he was often hungry; he would spend hours gazing at shops where clothes and food were offered, and longed to get his hands on some of the finery, and to sit down before a white tablecloth and eat and eat and eat.

In his heart he knew he would never be likely to do it. So his hatred burned more fiercely.

Then came the windfall.

Ben Marino, whose Italian extraction was so far back that he had nothing left of it but his name, brought the wind. Ben put occasional odd jobs in Bertie's way, and Ben came to him, one April evening when it was warm after a hot day and when Number 67 Bethel Street hummed to high heaven, with a suggestion, ten pounds, a small bottle of vitriol, and a promise of another fifteen pounds if Bertie did the job. All this was offered as Bertie leaned against the lamppost and Ben seemed only to pass the time of day. No one was within earshot.

If there lived anyone whom Bertie was willing to blind or scar for life, it was a policeman. He saw in this job an opportunity to avenge himself for every insult and injury. So Ben slipped him ten dirty pound notes, and went past quickly. That night— the night before the attack—Bertie had a blowout at Lyons' Corner House near Piccadilly Circus, went to the pictures and sat in the best seats, and glowed with satisfaction.

Next day, he did the "job."

That evening he was strolling toward the Blue Dog, the nearest public house to Bethel Street, and passing a certain doorway, when he heard his name called. It was Ben Marino. Ben often called him like this, seldom showed himself talking to the outcast.

Ben gave Bertie the extra fifteen pounds and a bottle of whisky and some good advice. He ought to have his drink at home, and lie low for a few days. The police hadn't a chance of catching him, but better be careful. He, Ben, would make sure that if there was any trouble, Bertie would be warned.

Bertie took his advice, and was soon back in the small, upstairs room. It had an iron bedstead, a heap of patched and torn blankets, a bamboo table, a wicker armchair, and a marble-topped washstand. The linoleum on the floor was wearing in patches, and a square of the window was covered with cardboard. He had two glasses; one of them wasn't cracked. He put this, a jug of water, and the whisky on the bamboo table, and sat back to enjoy himself.

Three-quarters of an hour later he was rolling drunk.

Three hours later he woke out of a stupor of sleep and knew there was something the matter. It was pain, in his stomach. He lay there, gasping, and a spasm of pain caught him and twisted, as if a hand were gripping his vitals. When it passed, he was sweating horridly, his face had a grayish pallor, and his limbs felt as if they'd turned to jelly. He groaned and tried to call out, but hadn't much voice. He hadn't the strength to get off the bed. He was fully clothed, except for his shoes.

Another spasm caught him; he gasped with anguish.

Not long afterward, he stopped gasping.

The police car drew up outside 67 Bethel Street, and Sloan and two Yard men got out. Divisional men who had been on watch farther along the street signaled that Bertie hadn't come out.

Sloan, standing almost as high as the door itself, knocked sharply on the iron knocker. There was no reply. He knocked again, and footsteps shuffled somewhere in the house. It was nearly midday, and warm; the smell from Number 67 ignored the wooden door.

This was opened by Ma Diggett, a slattern with gray hair which looked as if it hadn't seen brush or comb for a week. She clutched a threadbare coat round her pink flannelette nightdress, and looked at Sloan with bleary eyes.

"Who'ssat?"

"Police, Ma," said Sloan, and showed his card perfunctorily. "I want to see Bertie Downs."

"Why don'tcher leave 'im alone?" muttered Ma, but she opened the door wider, and stood aside. "Don't do no 'arm, Bertie don't, leave 'im alone."

"If he hasn't done any harm, we won't do any to him," Sloan said. "Go and wait in the kitchen, Ma."

She shuffled off.

Sloan led one man upstairs, and the other stayed by the door. No one had been in the street when they had arrived, except the Divisional men; there were now fifty people gathered round Number 67, from children in arms to septuagenarians. Anyone who joined that crowd was likely to have an easy conscience, Sloan knew; those who were scared of the police skulked behind closed doors, watching from behind curtains skillfully arranged so that they could see out without being seen.

Sloan reached Bertie's door, and thumped on it.

"Open up, Bertie, I want to talk to you."

There was no answer, no sound of movement.

Sloan knew that Bertie had come here last evening, and no one had seen him come out. He hadn't been in any of his usual haunts. It was possible that he had sneaked out after dark, and was in hiding; but Ma had seemed to think that he was still here.

Sloan banged again.

Then he gripped the handle of the door and put his shoulder to the flimsy panels. The door burst open.

He steadied himself as he lurched into the room,

44

heard nothing—and then saw Bertie stretched out on the bed. It wasn't a pretty picture. The window was closed tightly, there was no fresh air in the room, and the smell wasn't exactly like lavender.

Sloan stood quite still.

The Yard man with him said in a shaky voice, "Well, he won't give much away."

At the post mortem, they found enough arsenic in Bertie's stomach to have killed a dozen men.

6

Sick Leave

Roger sat back in a deck chair and watched Janet with the two boys, playing with an inflated Lilo on the beach near Alum Chine at Bournemouth. The Lilo, an air bed in gay colors, bobbed up and down on the gentle waves.

It was nearly four weeks since the attack, and except for three days of rain the weather had been perfect ever since. The shade temperature was well in the seventies today. Roger, with newspapers by his side, cigarettes on top of them, a beach hut behind him, felt dreamy and drowsy. The beach distracted his thoughts; he would get up in the morning, thinking of nothing but the latest news which Sloan wrote from the Yard, and come down here to yellow sandstone cliffs, topped here and there with pines, the fine, golden sand, the patches of pebbles, the distant views of the Purbeck Hills and of the Isle of Wight and the Needles—and begin to forget. The boys would grab their buckets and spades and rush to the sand, he and Janet would go down occasionally to join them.

He lit another cigarette.

Richard, who looked tiny in red swim trunks, and wore a pale blue shirt to protect his shoulders from the sun, came trailing across the sand and up the steps to the promenade, dragging his spade. He looked bored to distraction.

"Hallo, Daddy."

"Hallo, old chap."

Richard's blue eyes seemed to have taken color from the sky and the sea together. His ears stuck out and were slightly red from the sun, but in such a mood as this he had the face of an angel; and he was after something he didn't expect to get.

"Don't you want to play with the Lilo?"

"I'm getting tired of that," said Richard solemnly. "I'm hungry."

"That's bad."

Richard looked at Roger with passionate intensity, and asked: *"Can* I have an ice cream?"

Roger hid a smile. "Did you ask your mother?"

"No," said Richard.

"Sure?"

"Oh, I didn't, I promise," cried Richard, with the transparent honesty of his seven years.

"All right—buy one for Scoopy, too," said Roger, and handed over sixpence.

Richard lost his intensity, forgot to say thanks, started to run, turned, and shouted, *"Thank* you, Daddy!" over his shoulder, and went along without a worry in the world. Halfway toward the little café he stopped abruptly, and made a wide circle

47

round something Roger couldn't see. Then he ran on.

Roger suspected that he'd passed a large dog; he treated large ones with considerable respect. A moment later a mastiff came in sight, a huge beast straining at a leash; magnificent. The powerful front legs and shoulders, the blunt face, the sleek brown coat, drew everyone's attention.

A girl was holding on to the leash, right arm stretched out, as if she were having difficulty in keeping hold. She was tall and slim, and beautifully dressed in a cream-colored linen dress. She had slim legs and nice ankles, and wore red sandals; her toenails were not painted red. She wore a floppy hat with a red band, and huge sun glasses with red frames. She managed to create the impression that if she took off her glasses she would reveal the perfection of beauty.

She passed Roger without glancing at him.

Janet and Scoopy still played with the Lilo. A small boy moved toward them and stood watching. Janet spoke to him, and he joined Scoopy on the Lilo; a wave sent it shooting toward the beach, the boys crowed with laughter.

Roger glanced again toward the girl. She had turned back, and the dog was not pulling so hard. No doubt at all, both were magnificent. Two youngish men, approaching from the beach café, paused and watched the girl.

Richard appeared, licking one ice-cream cone and holding the other firmly. He was heading for the steps which led to the sands, and hadn't a care in the world. He hadn't seen the mastiff, which was fifty yards away from him.

Suddenly the girl cried, "Pete! Stop!"

The mastiff tore itself free and bounded, swift as light, toward Richard and the steps. Richard was close to them, and the cry had made him look round. Roger, already on his feet and moving, saw the terror which sprang into the child's eyes. Richard dropped the ice creams, threw up his hands, and stood still, as if paralyzed. An old man with a walking stick cried out and struck ineffectually at the mastiff.

It hurled itself at Richard.

Richard screamed, and went down. A woman shouted, the old man rushed nearer, beating the air with his stick, people on the beach stared, horrified, others jumped up from chairs outside the beach huts.

Roger passed the girl, who was running. He saw a confusion of Richard's brown arms and legs and red swim trunks, the dog, growling ferociously, only the old man daring to go near. The dog had Richard beneath its front paws, and was muzzling his face. There wasn't a sound from Richard.

A kick might make the brute slacken its grip, but would madden it. Roger straddled its back and bent down, burying his fingers into the thick neck, seeking the windpipe. He could feel the sinews and muscles, much stronger than his.

He gripped and pulled, and strained the dog's head back.

The girl came up, he saw her hat, her slim hands, and the leash. She gripped the leash and pulled.

"Pete, come off! Come off, understand? Come off."

The mastiff backed away; it was already clear of

Richard. She dragged it farther, a man said, "That dog ought to be put away." The beach superintendent came hurrying, and the crowd was now hundreds strong.

Janet was running from the sea, Scoopy trailing after her.

Roger picked Richard up. The boy's eyes were wide open, with a fixed look of terror. There was no blood; well, just a touch, where he'd grazed his hand on the path. The dog's teeth hadn't touched him. There was a smear of saliva over his hair, from the dog's mouth. His mouth was wide open.

He screamed again.

"Roger! What is it?" Janet flew to them, snatching the child away. "Richard, don't, it's all right, it's all right!"

Richard screamed once more, and then began to cry; a high-pitched, hysterical sound. Janet hugged him close, looking about her desperately. Scoopy came up and stared, round-eyed, thumb close to his mouth.

"Bring him to the first-aid tent," the beach superintendent said. "He'll be all right. This way."

Janet followed him; Richard's crying slackened, he began to sob more normally. Scoopy didn't know whether to go after him and his mother or to stay with Roger. The girl with the dog was some distance off now, and several people were standing about them.

The gray-haired man with the walking stick was saying:

"It's a crime to have a dog like that, it ought to be destroyed. If I were you, sir, I'd make a case out of this. Poor little chap, no wonder he was terrified. That brute—"

He broke off abruptly.

The mastiff pulled himself free again, and bounded toward the crowd. Children shouted, a girl screamed, Scoopy grabbed Roger's hand and gripped tightly. But the dog didn't worry about anyone on the promenade, he ran toward the road which led from the hill just beyond. A car had stopped there; a sleek, modern car. The girl ran after the dog, which made for the car and bounded in beside the driver. The girl reached them, jumped into the back, and the car moved off.

"Well!" gasped the old man. "She knew what was going to happen to it, if you got her name and address. But it won't be difficult to trace a brute like that. If I were you I'd go to the police right away."

"Yes," said Roger. "You've been very good."

"There's a telephone—"

"It's out of order," someone said. "I've just tried to make a call."

The car was at the top of the hill now, a dark blue Lagonda; a car Roger wouldn't forget in a hurry. Janet appeared suddenly at the entrance of the first-aid tent, which was among the bathing tents clustered together near the road and the car park.

Roger hurried, with Scoopy still holding his hand.

"Fetch his jumper and get the blanket from the car," said Janet. She looked pale but collected now, and there was no sound from Richard. "He'll be all right, but I want to keep him warm."

"I won't be long," said Roger, and turned. "Scoop, pop back to the hut and get Richard's jumper, will you?"

"*Must* I, Daddy?" Martin, called Scoopy, was a massive boy for his eight years, wearing only red trunks, and his body and limbs were bronzed and proof against the sun. He had a strong face and clear, frank gray eyes—which held Roger's.

It wasn't fair to send him alone.

"All right, old chap, come with me."

They ran toward the car park, which was just above the beach, built at the mouth of Alum Chine, a little valley running to the sea. Above were the cliffs; opposite was the road which led uphill into the suburbs and the town. Roger got the blanket and then hurried toward the beach hut, with Scoopy running alongside him. A few yards off shore the Lilo was bobbing up and down on the waves. The sun struck hot; Roger hadn't realized how hot it was. He stepped past the chair he'd been sitting in to get the jumper off a peg on the wall—and stopped.

On the small table inside was a thick, cream-laid envelope, bearing the typewritten address:

"Chief Inspector and Mrs. Roger West."

Roger felt suddenly cold.

Scoopy pointed to the jumper.

"There it is, Daddy, shall I get it?"

"Yes, please, old chap." Roger picked up the envelope and slipped it into his trouser pocket. Scoopy didn't see him. Scoopy pulled the jumper down, and turned to the door.

"We'd better hurry," he said, "or Mummy will be cross."

A woman from the next hut appeared.

"I'm so sorry, they've both been rather nervous of dogs, haven't they? It's too bad. Is there anything I can do?" She was middle-aged, plump, comely, and looked genuinely worried.

"I wonder if you'd go with Scoopy," Roger said eagerly. "Janet needs this."

"Of course I will."

He handed her the blanket.

"I'll show you where," said Scoopy, and led the way out of the hut. "Daddy, shall I tell Mummy you won't be long?"

"Yes, please, old chap," said Roger.

He kept a poker face until Scoopy and the woman had disappeared, took out the letter, then put it away hastily when someone else looked in; a man whose plump, amiable face was peeling badly from sunburn.

"It was disgraceful, that's what I say. I'd have the law on her, if I were you. The way she ran off, too —she knew what would happen if she didn't. It's criminal to have a dog like that."

"Yes," said Roger. "We'll find it."

It was five minutes before the man went. Outside everything was back to normal, the scene was tranquil, children were playing and shouting cheerfully, only one child was crying. A group in a yellow R.A.F. dinghy were splashing about a little way out to sea, and the Lilo lay floating between them and the sand.

That might be carried away.

Roger closed the doors of the hut, so that passers-by couldn't see him, and took out the envelope. He'd seen the other two; this looked as if it had been addressed on the same typewriter.

His teeth were clamped together as he tore it open.

There was a single fold of paper, exactly like the other two messages, and this one read:

You see what we mean.

7

Back on Duty

Roger put the note back in the envelope and pushed it in his pocket; Janet mustn't see that. He went out, and the woman from the next hut was coming back, and looking out to sea.

"Isn't that your Lilo?"

"Yes, but—"

"I'll tell my Sam to get it," said the woman, "you don't want to lose it."

She went to the edge of the promenade and called down to her lanky, ten-year-old Sam. Roger went toward the first-aid hut. No one was gathered round it now.

He pictured the running dog, the running girl, and the waiting car. He hadn't been able to see the driver clearly, and the girl had been disguised by the sun glasses; recognition would be almost impossible.

Richard was lying on a camp bed, round-eyed, looking quite normal. Janet sat by his side, and Scoopy was gazing rather wistfully out of the doorway.

"Hallo, Fish," said Roger cheerfully. "That was bad luck, wasn't it?"

"Yes," agreed Richard.

"I hate that dog," said Scoopy.

"Well, it didn't bite, you know," said Roger. "I shouldn't worry too much about it. Very few dogs bite people, especially children."

"At school, Michael Bligh said *he* was bitten by one," said Richard. "I don't like dogs."

"Do you still like ice creams?"

"Yes," said Richard firmly. "And I dropped mine." His voice quivered. "I didn't mean to, I—"

"Oh, it wasn't your fault," said Janet huskily. "Do you feel all right?"

"Yes, thank you—and I'm *still* hungry."

Richard threw off the blanket and sat up. One or two grazes showed red, but there were no teeth marks.

"Pop along together and get a sixpenny ice cream each," Roger said.

He gave Scoopy a shilling, and the two boys were half way to the café before they remembered to be nervous. They glanced round quickly, seemed reassured, and went on. Roger slid an arm round Janet's waist as they watched, and saw calm on her face again.

"It's a thousand pities it happened," she said. "They've never been very happy about dogs, but I thought they'd got over it. I suppose the only way is to get one ourselves. A puppy—"

"A puppy's no use," said Roger. "If we're going to have a dog, let's have a dog. We've always been against it because of week ends when we want to go away. After this, it might be the only way to stop them from being scared all their lives."

"I think we ought. That's if we can get one we can trust."

"I'll fix that," promised Roger.

Obviously Janet didn't dream that the attack had been planned. Roger walked with her behind the boys, who began to lick their ices and, finished, decided that it was high time they went back to the beach.

"Two more days," Janet said. "I'll be glad to get back, I think. I know you will!" She looked at the back of his hand, which was scarred but did not look too bad. "Is that really better, darling?"

"I don't feel a thing."

"Has Bill Sloan found out anything else?"

"Not yet," said Roger, and made himself sound casual. "I shouldn't worry about it, if I were you." He yawned. "I'm getting too lazy, here. I think I'll take a stroll. Coming?"

"We'd better not both leave the boys today, if they should run into another dog they'll panic," said Janet. "You won't be long, will you?"

"Just to stretch my legs," said Roger.

He had been sure that she wouldn't leave the boys by themselves.

He walked briskly to the road and turned into a hotel half way up, asked to use their telephone, and spoke to the Bournemouth police station. Ten minutes later a police car drew up and a brisk Detective Sergeant met Roger outside the hotel. Roger talked, and the sergeant made notes. There would be a search for the Lagonda and the mastiff; an immediate report to Scotland Yard; and, for safety's sake, a special watch on the small hotel where the Wests were staying, not far from this spot. Roger also handed over the letter.

"Oh, one other thing, if you will," said Roger. "Ask Sloan if he'll look out for a dog from the Training School. One used to children, if possible. Will you?"

"Gladly," promised the Bournemouth man.

During the next three days unhelpful reports came in about dark-blue Lagondas. None was reported with a mastiff as a passenger. The typewriter used for the third message was the same as that for the first two; tiny faults in two letters made that certain. The paper and envelope was of the same quality, but was sold widely throughout the country; by itself that wouldn't be a help. It carried no prints.

On the Sunday afternoon the Wests reached Bell Street again.

On the Monday Roger reported at the Yard.

"Hallo, young Roger," said Chatworth, at his most affable. It was nearly one o'clock, on that first Monday in May. "Glad you're back again, there's plenty for you to do. How's the hand?"

"I've almost forgotten there was any trouble."

"Don't forget too much." Chatworth lit a cheroot, and pushed cigarettes across the desk. "Sloan tells me you're going to have one of the dogs from the Training School. Very wise, I think. Better that kind of thing than send your family away, especially after what happened at Bournemouth. Satisfied with what Sloan's been doing?"

"I think he's done everything we can do yet. He's had full reports on the movements of Wiseman,

Gorley, and Kennedy, worked on the Bertie Downs angle which just petered out—if we could find out where Bertie got the money and the bottle of whisky it might help, but whoever did that was pretty slick," Roger said. "And he's faced a fact that I don't want to accept—that this is a deliberate vendetta. That's the part that doesn't make sense."

Chatworth said, "Why?"

"Look what's happened, so far. One man to toss the stuff at me. One to bring the letter to Bell Street. One to raid Mark Lessing's flat—that wasn't Downs, who couldn't pick a lock for a fortune, and he was probably dead at the time Lessing was visited. So whoever is behind it used at least three different people about the same time, and may have used more. At Bournemouth there was the girl, the car driver, the dog, and the Lagonda, and all of them spelled money. So whoever is behind it has plenty of cash—why waste it on getting himself back to jail?"

Chatworth grunted.

"I've told myself it might be an attempt to make us think it's a vendetta, and that there's something else behind it. I can't think what. Sloan had an idea," Roger added with a grin, "that I'd been following a case on the sly. I haven't—lately."

Chatworth let that pass.

"Looking at the three obvious possibilities, the least likely is Doc Gorley," Roger went on. "He's living with a drab, doesn't seem to have two pennies to rub together, and certainly hasn't been paying these people to have a cut at me."

"What about the others?"

"They've the money. They seemed to be living straight, although they're not exactly hiding their lights under bushels. Of the two Kennedy's the more likely, and Wiseman the more dangerous. Both made a habit of using stooges, neither did very much himself when he was working before, we had the devil's own job to get them."

"You got them," Chatworth reminded him.

"I was lucky. Lessing did a lot, too, and that's worth remembering," said Roger.

"Exactly what do you mean by that?"

"I'd like Lessing to have a free run on the job, he's nearly as deeply involved as I."

"I thought that was coming," grumbled Chatworth. "I don't like using amateurs and theoreticians, but if ever it were justified I suppose it is this time. Don't let him get out of hand. Remember he may have ideas, but he hasn't the training you and the others have. What about you? Want to take charge?"

"Please," said Roger.

"Well, mind yourself," Chatworth said, and waved dismissal.

During the next three days Roger checked everything that Sloan and Peel had done, but saw nothing they had missed. The accumulation of work kept him late at the office most nights, and threatened to for some time to come. He couldn't concentrate on the acid-throwing job; too much else demanded his attention. That was why he intended to use Mark. Mark could give the case all his time, the Yard had to spread their efforts.

Mark was busy making inquiries about Gorley,

Wiseman, and Kennedy. He reported to Roger each evening; nothing of consequence came up, but the list of friends and contacts of the three suspects grew larger.

On the fourth morning Sloan came into the office, grinning broadly.

"What's funny?" asked Roger, who was in his shirt sleeves and wrestling with a "suicide" which might prove to be murder.

"I've something for you downstairs. Can you spare a few minutes?"

"No." Roger stood up and put on his coat. They went out together. "Nothing to help, I suppose?"

"It depends on what you mean by help," said Sloan.

He turned down the stairs leading to the canteen, and two uniformed men passed. They looked startled. Sloan pushed open the door of the canteen and saw a dozen men standing at the bar, tea, cocoa, or sandwiches in their hands, staring at a creature which stood with head thrust forward, hackles up, and legs planted firmly. One of them moved a step, and the dog, an Alsatian standing higher than their knees, growled viciously.

A lean, gangling man standing behind the dog— everyone else was in front of it—called out: "All right, Snicker, they're friends."

The Alsatian stopped growling, and the hair on its back smoothed down. It strolled casually toward the man who had moved, and licked his hand. The lean man came forward and tickled it with the toe of his shoe.

"He's ticklish, too," he said. "Hallo, Handsome! This is the animal you asked us to get for you.

61

Tame as a white mouse when he's sure you're friends, but don't let him loose if you don't like the person you're with. Snicker! Say hallo to your new boss."

Snicker looked round; his head was magnificent, his ears were perked up, he looked from Sloan to Roger and back.

Roger moved forward.

"Friends, Snicker, your new boss," said the lean man.

The Alsatian nuzzled Roger's right hand.

"Get that brute out of here," said another man, swallowing half a sandwich. "I thought we were going to have to call the ambulance squad."

"He's as peaceful as a cooing dove, if you know how to handle him," asserted the lean man. "Just right for you, Roger. His last job was with the Ward children—remember the kidnaping scare? He had to look after them, and they discovered that he puts children first, adults afterward. Eh, old chap?"

Snicker stayed by Roger.

"You'll be all right," said the lean man cheerfully, "and you ought to hear him bark! He's perfectly house-trained, won't make a sound unless he hears someone in the garden or the house, and then he'll bring down the roof."

"He looks just right," said Roger, and quelled a doubt that Snicker was too large and ferocious-looking for the boys. "I'd better take him home."

"You're telling me," said the man who'd gulped down the sandwich.

"Think he's safe to take through the Yard?" asked Roger.

The lean man chuckled.

"He's as biddable as a lap dog. Try him for half an hour; if you have any trouble I'll come. He's been trained to the minute. He won't permit strangers anywhere near unless he's told it's all right, and if you use the two words 'get him'— he'll get his man. That's what he's been trained for."

"I'll chance it," said Roger. "Come on, Snicker."

Snicker rose from his haunches.

"Like company?" offered Sloan.

"You'd better keep in support." Roger led the way to the door, Snicker followed, Sloan brought up the rear. "Heel, Snicker," Roger said, and it made no difference; the dog kept by his side. "Get back, Snicker." Snicker looked up and, as nearly as a dog could, winked. "Behind me, Snicker."

Snicker stopped, as if he were drilling on the parade ground, fell in behind Roger, and walked sedately up the stairs and through the corridors of the Yard. Every man who passed stared; everyone looked back. Snicker took no notice of any, until a man who passed with a nod turned suddenly and shot out a hand.

"Oh, West—"

Snicker growled.

"What the hell's the matter with him?" The man glared.

"Just showing me what he can do," explained Roger. "All right, Snicker, friend. Yes?"

"I've just come in from the Divisions—A2." That was the Division where Bertie Downs had lived. "Old Charley there thinks he has a line on that chap Downs. Something to do with a man named

Marino. I've sent a note through, it might be worth following."

"I'll follow it—thanks."

The man went on, Snicker followed Roger into his office and, when told, went across to the window, lay down, stretched out his great body, and put his nose on his paws. He appeared to go to sleep. Roger sat at his desk, Sloan went out, and there was silence until a man passed the door. Snicker growled, stopping only when the footsteps had faded.

"He'll be just right." Roger moved, and lifted the telephone. Janet was soon on the line.

"Hallo, my sweet! I'm coming home to lunch—can you manage something?"

"Of course. It'll be cold, but I'll feed you," said Janet. "Why?"

"Remember we talked about a dog? He's turned up."

"Oh," said Janet, as if she were half-regretful. "I've talked to the boys about it, but they don't seem too keen. It's worth trying anyhow. Darling, have you heard from Mark?"

"Not this morning."

"He rang up just after ten, said he'd look in about twelve, and hasn't been," said Janet. "It's half-past twelve. I don't suppose it means anything, but I wondered if he'd been in touch with you. What time will you be in?"

"Not much after one," said Roger. " 'By, sweet."

He rang off.

Mark being late was hardly important; normally Roger wouldn't think twice about it. Yet he found himself thinking more about it than the possibility that a man named Marino could throw some light on the activity of Bertie Downs.

He telephoned A2 Divisions, but "Old Charley," the oldest Chief Inspector on the Force, was out.

Roger left the Yard for home at twenty to one, with Snicker at his heels.

8

Kennedy's Eve

Mark Lessing wrote Doc Gorley off as a dead loss.

The Doc—that was a courtesy title—had started life as an assistant to an East End chemist, acquired a little and more than usually dangerous knowledge of drugs, and soon afterward "practiced" on his own. A bland manner, an inflated ego, and a good line in talk had helped him to make a small fortune. Among the East End's poor he had thousands of "patients," many of whom swore by him. Eventually he had forged certificates and been accepted by the police as well as the public as a medical practitioner. He might still have been practicing, but for his greed. Where he made thousands of pounds, he wanted tens of thousands. He began to peddle drugs. Roger West had eventually had him sent down.

The Doc, a bulky man who at least had his bland manner left, lived only half a mile from Bertie Downs, with a woman he had known before his sentence. He spent most of his time at the nearest pub. The police watched him closely, to make sure that he didn't start dispensing medicines again. He picked up a living by doing odd jobs, including writing letters for illiterates, mostly colored and lascar sailors who planned to stay in England for a few years and thought it proper to write home. There, someone who could read would acquaint their wives and families. Occasionally, they sent money home; they knew the Doc well enough to send the money themselves—no one trusted him.

Mark felt sure that the possibility that Doc was behind the vendetta was negligible.

Soon after Roger had gone to hospital, Wiseman had gone to France, for a month at Cap d'Antibes. That was simply resuming a pre-prison custom. It might be significant that he had left England when the inquiries would be at their height; but the incident at Bournemouth had happened while Wiseman was away.

Mark, who normally divided his time between writing and attending Company meetings, for he was on the board of several small concerns, concentrated on Jacob Kennedy.

There were several angles. Kennedy had a luxury flat in a block of flats near Park Lane; a small wholesale business in the City, which his wife and two sons, Peter and Charles, had managed after he had been jailed; and a cottage near Guildford, in one of the loveliest parts of the countryside within easy reach of London.

Kennedy had resumed his normal life and mixed with most of the same people, the main social difference being that he was barred from his two West End clubs. There was little about Kennedy's life and movements Mark didn't discover in the month which followed the vitriol attack. Nothing led to the East End and Bertie Downs. Kennedy seemed to be leading an exemplary life.

It wasn't until after the Bournemouth incident that Mark really began to take an interest in Kennedy's secretary. Exactly what she did was something of a mystery. Cynics would have rejected that, but it was true. All indications suggested that Kennedy was happy with his wife. The girl, Eve Wedlake, had a small flat in Kensington, worked sometimes at the City office in Leadenhall Street, sometimes at Kennedy's flat, sometimes at the country cottage. She worked irregular hours.

To look at she was a dream.

In the late twenties, Mark judged, she had everything, including clothes sense. Her make-up was always just right, her carriage superb, her figure made men turn and glance at her, or else watch her furtively. She had fair hair and cornflower-blue eyes and an easy laugh; her voice was lovely.

Until the mastiff was let loose on Richard she was just Kennedy's secretary; Mark had a secret thought that it was a pity she had to work for the man. Afterward she became something else, because on that day in Bournemouth Eve Wedlake had officially been at the cottage. Mark had actually seen her drive off, in a small cream-colored two-seater, heading for Guildford which was on one main road to Bournemouth. He hadn't followed; it was one of the things he regretted most.

After that Mark spent a lot of time watching her and the rest of the Kennedy circle, and on the morning when he telephoned Janet he made an interesting discovery.

He was being watched himself.

The watcher had been outside his flat when he

had left, just after nine o'clock, had followed him to his garage, and driven after him in a small four-seater car, a black Austin ten. He had made no attempt to disguise the fact that he was interested in Mark.

He was a little man who wore a bowler hat and a shiny blue suit, and didn't seem to be the type who would mix with or work for Kennedy.

It was several days since Mark had been to Bell Street. He had intended going that morning. He telephoned Janet, said he would be in later, and then walked from the telephone kiosk near Piccadilly to his car, which was parked in a narrow side-street. The man in the bowler hat followed faithfully, and the Austin ten was just behind. Mark started off, drove slowly and with the main stream of traffic toward the Strand and the City at first, and then swung right, when traffic lights helped him, and scorched down to the Embankment. He watched his driving mirror closely; he had thrown off the Austin. He reached Blackfriars Bridge, turned toward Ludgate Circus and parked his car near St. Paul's.

He was no longer followed.

Mark's sleek green Jaguar was noticeable, even in London. He took a taxi to Leadenhall Street, where, he knew, Kennedy usually went in the mornings. He was there just after eleven o'clock. No one whom he recognized went in, but just after twelve, Eve Wedlake came out.

Usually she went to the parking place where she put her car. This morning she went in the opposite direction, past the tall, gaunt gray buildings of the City toward Liverpool Street Station. Mark followed at a distance. She turned into a café, one of a serve-yourself chain with a display of cheap food wrapped in cellophane in the window. Usually the girl had lunch at one of the City's more exclusive restaurants. Anyhow, it wasn't late enough for lunch. Mark sauntered past; would go in, if necessary. If she were going to meet the bowler-hatted man, and he rated that as a possibility, this would be just the place.

He didn't go in.

As he passed the front door, Eve Wedlake appeared from the shop, and smiled; there was no doubt the smile was intended for him. It was also intended to melt resistance. She had everything—and that morning it was sheathed in a green linen suit, beautifully cut, the latest from Hartnell. With it she wore a wide-brimmed, yellow linen hat, slightly aslant; and her hair was beautifully done.

"Good morning, Mr. Lessing," she said.

Mark stopped.

"Why, hallo." He was vague. "How are you?"

She had a smile which seemed to hold all the merriment in the world.

"I'm very well," she said. "Would you care to take me out to lunch?"

Mark gulped.

"And don't, please, pretend that you met me at a garden party or a night club, but can't quite remember my name. I'm Eve Wedlake. I work for Jacob Kennedy. I think it would be a good idea to have a talk. Of course, if you'd rather not—"

She paused, and her expression suggested that she couldn't imagine any man saying he would rather not dally with her.

"My dear Miss Wedlake, I'm—"

"Mrs. Wedlake," said the girl.

Mark said weakly, "Oh."

"Your detective service has let you down," said the girl lightly. "I was married during the war. My husband was killed in a raid over Germany, but I no longer grieve too much. I should hate you not to know everything about me."

"So should I," said Mark, and began to recover. "Where would you like to go? City, West End, or some little place in the country?"

"Not a little place in the country."

"Pity."

Mark turned, and she walked by his side toward the Bank of England. The pavement was crowded, they passed innumerable small shops, all of them appearing to do a flourishing trade. A barrow boy, his barrow piled up with oranges, was shouting incoherently. The newsvendors were calling hopefully. Eve Wedlake looked into Mark's eyes, and the glow of amusement in hers could easily have made a man feel a fool.

"Bringing the dog?" asked Mark, brightly.

She looked puzzled.

"Dog?"

"No poodle or lap dog or mastiff?"

"If you're going to talk much like this, luncheon ought to be stimulating," she said. "No, I haven't a dog. If I had, I certainly wouldn't take him to the office or to the flat—Mr. Kennedy doesn't like dogs."

"Poor chap," said Mark. "Well, it's his loss." He glanced round, did not think that they were followed, and waved to a taxi. It pulled up. "In you get," he said. "We'll go to Merry's and have a drink before we eat."

She sank back in the taxi. Every movement she

71

made seemed natural, and yet such grace wasn't quite natural. She had long, shapely legs, and the nylon was like a second skin. Her green shoes were trimmed with yellow; her handbag was of the same colors.

Mark took out cigarettes.

"Thank you," she said, and leaned forward to take a light. Her eyes were very clear and still smiling. "Are you puzzled, Mr. Lessing?"

"I get used to surprises. Nothing the great Jacob does will ever surprise me again."

"Won't it?" she asked, and there seemed to be an undercurrent of grimness in the words; the expression in her eyes altered for a moment, but the smile soon came back. "It must be dull, never to be surprised."

"Isn't life dull?"

"Usually I find it exciting."

"You would," said Mark. "Look at your start. I'm just a middle-aged bachelor keeping himself alive with his hobbies, while you have the advantage of youth, and lure of your sex. Did anyone ever tell you that you have everything?"

"A lot of people. They've never yet convinced me that they're right."

"Leave that to me," said Mark.

They talked on the same flippant note until they reached Soho. Here, in one of the little narrow streets, with a grocery and provision store on one side and a second-hand curio shop on the other, was Merry's. It was a single-fronted shop, with cream-colored net curtains stretched right across, and the name Merry's painted on the fascia board; nothing indicated that it was a restaurant. The moment they reached the door, however, it opened and a small gracious man in black clothes greeted them as if with real delight; this was Enrico, whose business it was to know every customer by name.

"Why, Mr. Lessing, I'm delighted to see you. Good morning, madam." He bowed slightly. "Would you prefer to be upstairs or down today, Mr. Lessing?"

"Could it be upstairs? In a corner?"

"Of course!"

"We'll have a drink first," said Mark, and Enrico led the way to a bar at the far end of the restaurant. This was not overcrowded with tables; only twenty could sit down at one time. Two tables were already in service; cutlery gleamed and the napery was snowy white. Half a dozen people were at the tiny bar, where a little Italian with a shock of dark hair beamed a welcome.

Eve Wedlake had a Manhattan.

They chatted.

Eve had another Manhattan.

They went upstairs.

The corner was secluded; no one else was within easy earshot. A small window overlooked the street, so a net curtain was drawn across it, because Enrico did not think that the drab view could possibly help anyone to enjoy food cooked more perfectly here than anywhere else in London. He said that himself—truthfully, not boastfully.

He took their order, advised this and advised that, the first course came up, and he withdrew, with the waiter.

Mark spread *pâté* on buttered toast.

"Now what is this all about?"

The girl laughed.

"You've been very patient, but Jacob said you would be. He has a very high opinion of you, Mr. Lessing."

"Doesn't Jake Kennedy call me Mark?"

"No," she said, and her eyes brimmed over with merriment.

"Couldn't you?" pleaded Mark.

"I'm beginning to believe that what he said about you was justified."

"Oh, come." Mark was shocked. "I'm not as bad as all that."

"He has nothing but good to say of you. If you think that he bears some malice, you're quite wrong. He gambled and lost. In the dock he said some foolish things about you and Roger West, but he soon forgot that. He's paid his losses now, and he's all square. He's puzzled about you, of course."

"Naturally."

"He can't understand why you're taking such an interest in him," said Eve.

"And you're to find out?"

"If I can," said Eve. "Because he thinks it possible that you'll be able to help him."

9

Proposition

Eve delivered her bombshell with serene aplomb, spread *pâté* over toast, and looked into Mark's eyes as if that were what she wanted to do more than anything else in the world. They had been together now for little more than an hour; she had already contrived to make him feel as if they were old friends, and that he really mattered to her. It wasn't what she said or how she said it; it was a peculiar atmosphere she created; and Merry's contributed an indefinable something.

"Really," said Mark at last. "I can't imagine anyone I'd like to help less than my old pal Jacob Kennedy."

"You shouldn't think like that."

"You see, I don't think he's a nice chap."

"He is, when you get to know him. He's a big gambler, and doesn't care a snap of the fingers for the law—although he'll make sure he never does anything outside it again, he's learned that lesson —and he bears no malice. I hope you won't."

"Well, well," breathed Mark. "So poor Jacob's

been misunderstood all these years. I'll have to tell Roger West that, he hasn't had many laughs lately."

"Wasn't he hurt, or something?"

"Slightly," said Mark. "It made him angry."

"Really?" Eve shrugged. "I wish you'd change your attitude about Jacob Kennedy. Why are you watching him?"

She put her knife on her plate and finished the *pâté*.

The waiter hovered nearer, took the plates away, and while they were waiting, Mark offered cigarettes.

"American habit," he explained.

"I won't smoke now," said Eve. "Why are you watching Jacob?"

"Eve the Persistent! To tell you the simple truth, someone with a grudge is having a cut at Roger West and me." If she already knew, or guessed, she would surely show some sign; she showed only mild surprise. "In fact, the said someone bribed the boy who tossed the vitriol. Don't tell me you don't remember exactly what happened."

She looked—horrified.

"What?"

"Sorry you're so sensitive," said Mark. "It's a fact. Someone with a deep grudge tried to disfigure Roger, and has played one or two other little tricks. The one at Bournemouth, for instance."

Her expression didn't change, Bournemouth seemed to hold no special significance for her.

"Are you sure about this?"

"Oh, yes."

"And you think—" She caught her breath. Either it was acting worthy of the stage, or she was genu-

76

inely horrified; had it been any other method of attack, such horror would have seemed overdone; but vitriol-throwing affected many people like that. "And you think that Jacob had something to do with it?"

"He could have."

"He has not!" She was almost angry. "It's a foul suggestion to make."

"It was a foul thing to do."

The waiter came up, with fillets of Dover sole in a sauce which could not be made anywhere but at Merry's. As it melted in their mouths, and they looked at each other, the girl's annoyance seemed to fade. By the time they had finished she was back to normal; or nearly normal. She was no longer smiling with her lips or with her eyes.

"And you are looking for whoever did it?" she said.

"Brilliant deduction!"

"It was not Jacob Kennedy."

"Good."

"You don't believe me, do you?" she asked.

"Oh, I wouldn't go so far as that. Jacob's only one of several possibilities. If he could convince me that he's really reformed, doesn't bear any malice, and would like to be my bosom friend—and Roger's—I might begin to believe that he's about one-tenth as good as you say he is. Eve, I don't know a thing about you, but you look a nice girl. You talk like a nice girl. Be warned—Jacob Kennedy is a bad man."

Eve flushed, and didn't answer.

"A very bad man," insisted Mark.

She looked at him steadily.

"I think you are quite wrong. I have worked for

him for six months now, and have discovered nothing but good. His wife and two sons are nice people, too. Jacob has a different sense of what is right and wrong, that's all—he freely admits that. He thinks that currency regulations are—"

"A lot of people cock a snook at currency regulations. Only the really nasty types use blackmail."

"He was wrongly charged with blackmail."

"Judge and jury considered it proved."

"Then the judge and jury were wrong."

"Well, Jacob's had one slice of luck," said Mark sadly. "A lot of men would give their right hands to have you as loyal as that. He must have a very nice side to show to his secretaries. Let's call a truce. What's he doing these days? Making millions?"

"He's making money."

"Who's surprised?"

"And he is being blackmailed," said Eve Wedlake quietly. "He has been threatened several times, and is beginning to fear that his life is in danger. Because of what happened in the past, he's been reluctant to report it to the police. He doesn't think that the police will take him seriously, or care what happens to him. His wife and I persuaded him to let me talk to you about it. He hates to admit it, but he's badly in need of help, and the only people who can really help him are the police. Will you tell Roger West that?" When Mark made no answer, she leaned forward, rested the tips of her fingers on the back of his hand, and went on, "If you can make him help, will you? Jacob says that next to the police, he believes that you're most likely to be able to find who is behind this trouble. Of course, he doesn't think you'll try," she added, and pressed his hand gently. "He's quite sure that

78

he'll get no sympathy from you or from the police. You'll say he's asked for everything he's got, but—*I* don't think he's right. Is he?"

At half-past two they left Merry's. There was no sign of a man with a blue suit and a bowler hat; only a few people, mostly poorly dressed inhabitants of the district, were in the street. They had to walk for five minutes before a taxi came along.

Mark put the girl into it.

"I know I haven't convinced you," she said, "but at least it's something to think that you're prepared to talk to Roger West about it, and will meet Jacob. Get in touch with me, not with Jacob, won't you?" Amusement glowed in her eyes. "You know where I live!"

She sat back.

Mark closed the door, told the driver where to go, paid him in advance, and watched the taxi out of sight. Two or three more hours in Eve Wedlake's company, and he would begin to believe that black was white and that Jacob Kennedy's return to freedom had been heralded by angels' trumpets.

The girl didn't look back.

Mark took another cab to the City, picked up his car, and drove to Chelsea. It was nearly four o'clock before he arrived. The front door was open, but there was no sign of Janet; the boys wouldn't be home yet. He hurried along the path, suddenly nervous; it was still hot, but would Janet leave the door wide open, invitation to any who wanted to come? He didn't wait in the porch, being used to going in and out of the house as he liked, but a fierce growling stopped him in the doorway.

He stood rooted to the porch.

An Alsatian, huge and powerful, stood at the foot

of the stairs, teeth bared, hackles up. Mark felt his heart pounding. The trick with Richard and the mastiff might have been repeated. He took a step forward, and the dog growled more ferociously, and crouched as if to spring. Mark knew what would happen if he went on, but didn't know what would happen if he turned his back on the brute.

He backed a pace; the dog just glared.

"Janet!" called Mark. It wasn't like his voice to sound thin and uncertain.

"Who—oh, Mark!" Janet's voice came from the head of the stairs, a tremendous relief, and she hurried into sight. "I thought I heard Snicker. All right, Snicker, he's a friend. Come in, Mark."

"Come *in?* Past that?"

"He won't hurt you now. Try it."

Janet looked her best. Inevitably Mark compared her with Eve Wedlake; neither really suffered against the other. He went forward gingerly, and Snicker came to meet him, teeth no longer bared and his coat smooth. Mark gulped, as the dog nuzzled his hand.

"Nicely trained," he said.

"It's a police dog, Roger brought him. Mark, you couldn't have come at a better time. Will you meet the boys from school and tell them we've a dog? Then I can be waiting with him, and introduce them."

"Yes, of course." Mark was dubious. "But if he turns as friendly as that at a word—"

"Only to those who've been introduced."

"I have great faith in the intelligence of dogs, but there are limits," Mark said. "I'll fix the boys. Sorry I couldn't get here earlier, I had an unexpected date."

"Roger said it was nothing to worry about," said Janet. "I'll telephone and tell him you've turned up. The boys should be ready to leave school in about five minutes," she added.

"I'll hurry," promised Mark.

Richard and Scoopy listened, thoughtfully, to the story of the dog—a large dog—and when they reached the house, Richard's hand slid into Mark's. They approached timidly. As they entered the porch, Janet appeared, with Snicker by her side. Scoopy drew back involuntarily, and Richard's fingers tightened on Mark's hand and he pressed against Mark's legs. Snicker did not growl, but licked his lips.

"Friends, Snicker," said Janet. "This is Richard and Scoopy, and you're going to have a wonderful time together. He's used to children, boys, you'll love him! Go and say hallo, Snicker. Say hallo, boys."

The dog came forward.

Richard's whole body was taut, like wire; and he didn't move. Scoopy shot a glance at his mother, as if to make sure that she was serious; then confidence that she wouldn't let him down overcame his fears, and he stretched out his right hand. Snicker nuzzled the fingers, pushed past him, and stood a foot or two in front of Richard. Janet didn't speak; Mark kept silent.

"He's all right," said Scoopy, with sudden pride. "*I* let him touch me, didn't I, Mummy? He's a nice dog. I like him. Is he mine?"

"Ours," said Janet softly.

Richard said. "He's *very* big." To the child he

must have seemed enormous. "Ever so big," Richard added, and moved an inch or two.

Snicker, as if sensing his nervousness, stood where he was; Richard put out his hand and touched his coat, and Snicker wagged his tail.

Ten minutes later, over a cup of tea, Mark and Janet watched the two boys on the back lawn, with Snicker chasing after a red ball.

"That's one worry over," Janet said, and her tone betrayed the extent of her relief. "Mark, what happened today?"

"I'll come back this evening and tell Roger, you can listen to the whole story. If Roger gets here before I do, tell him Jacob Kennedy has turned over a new leaf, will you?" Mark chuckled, and left soon afterward.

He drove straight to his Victoria flat, passed the building, saw no one, and wondered if the man in the bowler had given him up as a bad job. He put the car in the garage, and strolled back to the flat. A woman and two children were approaching from the far end of the street, a big Buick hummed past Mark. He was thinking of Eve Wedlake and wishing she wasn't quite what she was; it would be easy to let her fool him, hard to believe that she was bad.

Although she worked for Kennedy, she didn't have to be bad; the man might have fooled her.

He laughed at himself.

He reached the landing of his flat, thoughts switching to the Wests, the dog, and the boys. If the show broke the boys of their nervousness of dogs, it would be one good thing. Was it possible that they were making too much of it? Had he wasted his time?

He opened the door and went in—and a man stepped forward from the side of the room. Mark saw the gun in the man's hand, opened his mouth to shout—and saw a cloud of vapor come from the gun. As the first sound reached his lips, the vapor bit at him—sharp, agonizing. It was as if his face and eyes were on fire, his nostrils and mouth seemed scorched. Tears flooded his eyes, he was mute and blinded, struck out wildly but touched nothing and saw nothing.

A door banged.

He staggered forward toward the piano, fell against it, heard the muted twanging of the wires, and stayed there, with tears streaming down his face and the pain more agonizing than ever.

10

Gas

Mark leaned against the piano, his face still burning, panic in his mind. He fought against it. No liquid, only gas had come from the gun. Remember that, hold it fast, remind himself that it wasn't acid, but—

Gas.

He clamped his teeth together.

His eyes hurt more than anything else, and he couldn't see; he kept opening them, but there was only a blur. He moved slowly, stopped, made himself remember exactly where he was. Panic wouldn't help. He was leaning against the back of the piano. If he stepped forward, turned right, and then veered right, he would come to the fireside chair and the telephone on the table.

Tears streamed down his cheeks.

He stood up, drew himself to attention, took two steps, and turned right; he banged into the piano. New pain was added, it went right through him. He rubbed at his thigh, and gradually it eased. He took another step and then turned right and began to grope. Blind, useless idiot—he'd lived here for ten years and couldn't find his way about! Now he wasn't quite sure where he was. Right or left? He took another step forward, kicked a table, and a bell rang faintly; that was the telephone table.

He couldn't be too bad, or he wouldn't have the sense or the nerve to do this. He felt the shiny surface of the telephone, picked it up, then stopped abruptly; how could he dial when he could not see the numbers? He caught his breath. His mouth seemed parched, as if a fire had burned all the moisture out of it. He spoke aloud and managed only a croaking whisper. He nearly dropped the telephone, steadied himself, and dialed O. That was the last letter on the dial, and easy to find. He heard the ringing sound.

A girl said, "Operator, can I help you?"

Mark croaked, "Send—doctor—18c Crane Court, Candor Street, Victoria. Can—you—hear?"

The girl's manner changed completely; she was no longer brisk and aloof.

"Yes, sir, I have the message, I'll send for a doctor immediately. 18c Crane Court. Is there anything else I can do?"

"Connect me—Scotland Yard. Chief Inspector—West."

"Hold on one moment, sir, please."

He held on, swaying; his voice must sound better over the telephone than it did to himself. The waiting seemed agelong; then he heard Roger's voice.

"Hallo, who's that?"

"Mark," Mark croaked. "Flat—hurry."

"Ten minutes," said Roger, and banged down the receiver.

Mark found his lips curving into a smile; ten minutes—and it would probably be less. It wasn't far from the Yard to his place. Trust Roger; you could always trust Roger. You could always be sure that he, Mark Lessing, would make a fool of himself sooner or later.

That girl; Eve.

Had she anything to do with this? Was she a Delilah? Hardly that—Circe, more like. It didn't matter. He felt dizzy, and the strange dryness of his mouth and nostrils worried him. It hadn't been acid, but gas could do—

It couldn't be too serious, or he wouldn't have had the strength or the nerve to do what he had. No, it wasn't too bad. He staggered away from the table, groped for and found an armchair, and dropped into it. The door would still be open—

Would it? The man who had spurted that gas at him might have closed it; yes, a door had banged. Roger had a key; Roger had everything.

No, Eve Wedlake had everything.

Mark giggled, stopped, felt a sudden despair; because he couldn't see. He was sitting back in his own hide armchair and couldn't see. Did shock do things like this to you?

Mark heard the key turn in the lock, then heard footsteps, and half-rose from his chair. More footsteps followed, and then he heard Roger's voice.

"Hallo, old chap!" Cool and calm, as you'd expect from Roger. The footsteps were no more hurried than the voice. "All right, Bill, get moving," Roger said; so that meant that Bill Sloan had come with him. Next moment a hand fell on

Mark's shoulder. "It's all right, could have been a lot worse. Ammonia—gas or liquid?"

Ammonia!

"Are you—sure?" squeaked Mark.

"It smells to high heaven," said Roger. A window was flung back, and another, and a cool breeze blew through the room. "I shouldn't think it's done much harm. Better let me bathe your eyes. The girl told me you'd sent for a doctor—he'll be here in a few minutes."

"Ammonia," said Mark disgustedly. "I thought it was mustard gas at least. I'm—"

He broke off.

"You'll do fine. Did you see who it was?"

"Just. Tallish chap. No bowler hat."

"No what?"

"Bowler hat or blue suit. I didn't tell you about him, did I?" Mark caught his breath, then said with great deliberation, "No, I am not driveling or delirious. I'll make sense of it in a minute. I—"

A voice came from the door. "Is this where you want a doctor?"

"Come right in," said Roger. "You've been quick. Thanks."

Trust him to say the right thing at the right time.

The doctor's voice was youthful and his manner reassuring.

Mark sat back in his armchair, over an hour later, and looked at Roger. He couldn't see well, and his eyes kept blearing over, but he could recognize Roger, and was now prepared to believe that after a night's sleep he would be as good as new. He felt physically limp; exhausted. He didn't want

87

to smoke, because of the foul taste in his mouth, and yet he had an urge to smoke. By his side was a glass of milk with some powders in it; the doctor, having prescribed it, had gone.

Sloan and another Yard man had left the flat.

Roger handled an envelope, with a single fold of cream-laid notepaper.

"So we had another one," said Mark heavily.

"Reminder number four," Roger nodded. He glanced down and read, " *'You meddle too much— don't.'* Short and sweet," Roger remarked. "No prints, nothing to help identify the thing except the same defects on the typewriter, no doubt it was written on the same machine. It was on top of the piano. Whoever it was forced that door lock without any difficulty again, he's getting used to it. The street door was open, wasn't it?"

"Always is, during the day." Mark dabbed at his eyes and sipped his milk. "I suppose—"

He broke off.

"Suppose what?"

"Could it mean I've been getting near?"

"Yes, but it needn't," said Roger. "I called Janet just before you rang through, and she gave me a cryptic message." He sat back expectantly. "Had any luck?"

Mark forced a grin.

"It depends what you call luck." He leaned forward, sipped his milk again, and began to talk. He wasn't in his best form at storytelling, and the narrative took twenty minutes; he felt vaguely dissatisfied with what he had said, and as he finished, forced a laugh and added, "Mind you, I haven't done Eve Wedlake justice."

"I've had one or two reports about her," said

Roger with a crooked smile. "She seems to knock everyone cold."

"She could be the girl of the Bournemouth promenade."

"Oh, yes," said Roger.

"Seen her yourself?"

"Not yet, but I'm going to soon."

Roger took out a cigarette, then put it away.

"Oh, smoke," said Mark.

"It won't do me any harm to cut down. So we have a pretty picture of Jacob Kennedy in trouble but lacking the nerve to appeal to the police. That rings false, if anything ever did—he has nerve enough for anything. It might be a good idea to pretend to fall for it, though."

"I fancied you'd think so." Mark was regretful. "I thought you'd probably ask me to take her out to dinner so that we could have another cozy chat, but I couldn't make the grade tonight. Will you go and see her?"

"She was anxious that you should tell her, not go straight to Kennedy, you say."

"Yes."

"I think I'll go and meet the lady," said Roger. He stood up, and put his head on one side. "You're looking much better, you'll probably be quite over it by the time you go to bed. If I have any luck with Eve I'll come and tell you. Or—better still, go and see Janet, and wait—"

"No." Mark was emphatic. "It'll worry her to know it's still on the go."

"It'll worry her more if she finds out afterward that we've been keeping this back," said Roger. "This isn't in the same class as the Bournemouth show, I didn't want her to think that there might be any danger for the boys. I should go along, I think. I'll tell a man to drive you, and I'll bring you back later, myself."

"Maybe you're right," Mark conceded.

"I'll tell the man to be ready when you are," Roger said.

He went downstairs, had a word with one of the men on duty in the street, and got into his own car, a green Morris 14, with a supercharged engine. He drove toward Kensington, then approached Worrall Street, where Eve Wedlake lived. He didn't turn into it, but stopped a hundred yards away, lit a cigarette, and stared along the street, where lights were showing faintly yellow against the gathering dusk. It was nearly eight. He drew hard at the cigarette and let thoughts trickle through his mind. The unknown enemy was shrewd and clever, and was playing a war of nerves. He was doing it well, too. If there were anything really surprising, it was that he had taken such risks and done so little. Comparatively little, anyhow; the nearest to a serious attack had been the vitriol. Thereafter it had been pin-pricking, but pin-pricking in the most painful places. The police were no nearer finding out who he was than they had been a month before.

The one hope was through the man Marino, but that was pretty thin. Old Charley had told him that Marino had been noticed talking to Bertie Downs, on the evening before the attack. They'd had a minute's talk outside Bertie's house, and the informant, a squealer well known to the Division and usually reliable, said that Marino had handed something over to Bertie. That proved nothing; it might be worth pulling Marino in, but that could easily be the wrong tactics. Roger had decided to let Marino ride, and just have him watched.

This job was going to take some time.

He let in the clutch at last, and drove along to Worrall Street. It was a short street of red-brick houses, several of them with *Apartment* or *Furnished Flat* signs hanging outside or in the windows. If you flew across Kensington and dropped a dozen pebbles out of the plane, you could be pretty sure that six of them would land in streets like Worrall Street. Number 17 was exactly the same as the others; tall—at least four stories, and the dormer windows at the top might mean there was a fifth—with red brick weathered to a browny color, four steps leading up to a massive front door. The paint could do with touching up, but wasn't really in bad condition. The sign outside was *Furnished Service Flats. Vacancies.* He left the car ten yards from the front door and walked back to it. The front door was open; that was quite usual. As he went up, an elderly woman appeared from the right, and waited for him.

"Good evening," she said.

"Good evening." Roger smiled. "Is Mrs. Wedlake in?"

"I don't know," said the elderly woman, in a voice which suggested that she hadn't much time for Mrs. Wedlake. "I was just coming to shut the door, it ought to be locked after dark. I'm not sure it's wise to leave it unlocked by day, either."

"I couldn't agree with you more," said Roger. "Which is Mrs. Wedlake's flat?"

"Top floor, on the right," said the elderly woman grudgingly. "No, the left."

Roger beamed at her. "Thank you so much."

91

He ran lightly up the stairs, humming under his breath. He'd studied two reports on Eve Wedlake, and his own men had been as impressed as Mark; and Mark wasn't usually impressed by a girl. She seemed to have a good mind, too, and a sense of humor.

He stopped at the third landing; there were two doors, and the only light came from the landing below. He found the switch and pressed it down. A card in a bracket on the nearer doorway read: Miss Ethel Swan. He turned to the other doorway, and saw what looked like a white envelope stuck on, with a pin; possibly a message to callers, to say she was out.

He drew nearer.

It was a message, but it wasn't from the girl. It was typewritten on the envelope, which was of familiar cream-laid pattern, and it said:

Don't see too much of Lessing.

11

Kennedy

Roger read the brief message again, and began to smile. The *i* and the *e* were slightly broken, it had been typed on the same machine as the others. It was clever; too clever? His smile broadened as he looked round the landing. It was bare; only an old blanket box stood at the top of the stairs, close to the wooden banisters. Roger went and sat down, crossed his legs, and looked round mechanically for an ashtray. There wasn't anything that would serve. He took out a penny, squashed the butt of a cigarette on it, sat for ten minutes without smoking, then lit another cigarette.

He heard footsteps downstairs. Two women spoke, a door opened and closed, and a single set of footsteps continued. He moved from the chest to a recess, where it was shadowy and he was less likely to be seen. He was anxious to see this wonder girl himself.

Another door on the landing below opened and closed; there was a moment's silence, then radio music sounded clearly. He shrugged and went back to his seat. He would give Eve Wedlake an hour; it would be worth that, to see her expression when she read the message.

He was beginning to put his money on Kennedy; there was something characteristic about this affair which reminded him of the earlier Kennedy case. Jacob had been too clever, too tortuous, in that. It mustn't be forgotten.

There was a sound, outside; like a car backfiring. Roger got up slowly, his ears strained—and the explosive sound came again. He moved toward the stairs swiftly and ran down them, and as he reached the next landing a new sound came from the street—a scream. A third report came more clearly through an open window; that wasn't a backfire; that was a gunshot. He heard more screaming and shouting, followed by a crash. There had been a background sound of a car engine, all the time.

The radio music went on and on. A door opened downstairs, as Roger reached the ground floor. A car engine roared, and a police whistle shrilled out, familiar, welcome, unmistakable. The elderly woman who had admitted Roger stood by the door of her flat, mouth stiffly open.

"Did you hear—"

Roger opened the door and rushed into the street.

A policeman flashed by, clinging to the open door of a car. Another car was at the end of the street, and Roger saw it swing round the corner, toward the High Street. A third followed the second, also with a policeman on the running board.

A dozen people stood about, and two were by the side of a small cream-colored two-seater, which had crashed against a lamppost. The lamppost was bent, the top drooped down, but the electric light was still on. It shone upon the girl who sat at the wheel of the car, and the man at her side.

The man was handsome, bareheaded, and looked unconscious. He was Jacob Kennedy.

One of the couple bending over the girl said reassuringly: "It's all right, not much harm done."

He opened the door, and helped her out. She looked dazed. Her hat was askew, and she pushed her hair back from her forehead. The street lamp light shone upon her beauty; disheveled as she was, Roger knew exactly what the others had meant when saying that Eve Wedlake had everything.

She swayed as the man helped her out of the car.

Doors were opening, people streaming into and along the street. The cars had disappeared, the only sound of engines came from a long way off. Voices made a constant chatter of meaningless sound.

Roger went to the other side of the car, and helped a man to raise Kennedy up from his seat. Kennedy was a dead weight, and his eyes were still closed.

"Better get him out," the other man said.

"Be careful with him, please." That was the girl, anxiously. "He may have been wounded."

"No blood," said the man who was helping Roger. "They got a damned sight nearer me than they did him. I'd like a word with them!"

He didn't pay any further attention to the girl, but put an arm behind Kennedy, and eased him forward. Roger helped to lift the man from the car and to the pavement.

"See, no injury," said the passer-by. "Shock, that's all. Live near here?"

"I do, he—" Eve began.

"He'll be round in a few minutes and can get upstairs under his own steam," Roger said.

He took a hip flask from his pocket, unscrewed it, and pressed the cap against Kennedy's lips. The man gulped a little whisky, and the muscles of his neck moved.

"See," said the passer-by.

"I'll go and open the door," said Eve.

She turned and hurried into the house. The elderly woman stood in the doorway, and exclaimed: "Well!"

Accusation, reproach, and "I-told-you-so" were all in the one word.

Eve ignored her, but had to pause. That gave Roger time to follow her, and he was just behind her when she started up the stairs. He walked silently, she made plenty of noise. Twice, as she turned a bend in the stairs, she might have seen him; she didn't appear to, but looked straight ahead of her. She clutched the banister rail, as if she needed support; and although the light was poor, she showed every symptom of suffering from severe shock.

She stopped on the landing, put a hand to her forehead, and swayed; Roger was almost stirred to go forward to help her. He didn't. She squared her shoulders, fumbled with her handbag, and took out the key. He was standing near the recess, and could only see her profile—but that was enough. She saw the message, thrust her head forward, read it—and stiffened.

The key dropped from her fingers.

She didn't utter a sound, just stood swaying, with one hand at her forehead. Then she turned. Had she looked up, she would have seen Roger. She didn't, but groped for the key. It was only a few inches away from her foot, but she seemed to have difficulty in focusing her gaze, and seconds passed before she picked it up. It trembled in her fingers. The key grated against the outside of the lock; it seemed an age before she inserted it, and turned.

She didn't take the message down.

She opened the door wide, swayed again, and, with a hand at her forehead, went in.

As she went, a man leaped at her out of the darkness of the room, hand raised, a weapon in it. Eve stood as if mesmerized, not even raising her arms.

The man had a gun.

Roger roared, *"Drop it!"*

He startled the man and made him swing round. The girl swayed sideways, struck the doorpost and leaned there. Roger ducked. The man squeezed the trigger, and a white vapor billowed out from it. He'd squeezed too soon, he was two yards away. He realized that, and snatched at his pocket, as if for another weapon.

Roger leaped at him, head bent, butted him in the stomach, and sent him reeling back into the room. The light was poor here. Roger straightened up, saw the gas pistol on the floor, and a blackjack in the man's hand. He struck savagely for the chin, then for the stomach and for the chin again. The man crashed down, and the blackjack fell to the carpeted floor.

Roger straightened up, rubbing his knuckles, turned round, and switched on the light.

The girl had moved from the doorway, and stood leaning against the back of a chair in a lounge hall, comfortably furnished and decorated with taste. She seemed to be making a great effort to recover her self-control, and moistened her lips before saying: "Are you—all right?"

"Yes, thanks. Go and open a window, will you, and all the doors."

The smell of ammonia was powerful here; it was worse on the landing. Roger's eyes were stinging and beginning to water. The girl went across the lounge hall and opened all the doors, and a moment later he heard windows opening.

The man on the floor didn't stir.

He was tall and lean, with a trilby hat which had fallen some feet away, and a light-colored raincoat, with the collar turned up. He also wore a choker. It had been pulled up over his mouth and chin, but had fallen round his neck now. He had a thin face, a long nose, and sandy-colored hair which grew well back on his forehead. His mouth was slack; he looked more dead than alive.

Eve came back.

"If you hadn't—" she began.

"Forget it," said Roger. "I'm West, of the Yard. Go downstairs and ask one of the policemen to come up here, will you?"

She didn't move.

"*You're* Roger West?"

"Yes." He smiled. "No ogre."

She didn't speak. The ammonia gas hadn't affected her much, her eyes were watering slightly, but that only made them seem more brilliant. Her make-up was perfect, and the way her hat had been pushed to the side of her head and her hair ruffled gave an added touch of attractiveness; she looked a natural beauty.

"All right," she agreed. "I'll go down."

"And say nothing about this," he said. "Please. Not even to Kennedy."

"All right."

She didn't ask why, but went out.

Roger bent down, dragged the unconscious man by the shoulders into another room, and went across to the open window. He could hear the sound of voices traveling up from the street below. He left his victim so that he could keep an eye on him, and also watch the street. By peering out he could see the pavement immediately outside the house, the two-seater, which had been shifted in to the curb, the crowd now fifty or sixty strong, and Kennedy, with a man bending over him; he couldn't be sure whether Kennedy was conscious or not.

Eve appeared, went straight to a constable, and spoke in a voice which Roger couldn't hear. The man looked surprised, but moved to the front door at once, and disappeared.

The man on the floor stirred.

Eve looked at Kennedy, but didn't go near him; the man bending over him was probably a doctor; a car stood near by. The cackle of voices sounded clearly, newcomers joined the crowd, and words floated up.

"He was shot."

"A machine gun, I think."

"Don't talk rot."

"Well, there was a lot of shooting."

"*I* only heard three shots."

The policeman reached the landing and peered into the flat.

"Are you there, Mr. West?"

"Yes, come in." Roger stepped over the prisoner's body, as the constable reached the middle of the lounge hall. "Keep an eye on this chap, will you? He's violent, don't let him start any rough stuff. Get him into a chair, if you can, facing the door, and see that the door's closed. All clear?"

"Yes, sir, thanks."

"Good man," said Roger. "I won't be long."

He hurried down the stairs, but didn't join the group on the pavement. He stopped where he could see the girl. She was still some distance from Kennedy, and he was pretty sure that she hadn't said anything to the man, who was conscious; the doctor straightened up from him, and said: "You'll do. Better get home and go to bed. A night's sleep will put you right."

Eve moved forward.

"Need an ambulance, sir?" asked a sergeant.

"Oh, no. Car will do." The doctor was brusque. "You know where to find me." He handed the man a card. "I must hurry."

He walked to his car, which was on the other side of the road, and drove off.

"If we could get him up to my flat, he could rest there," said Eve.

"You were driving the car, Miss, weren't you?" That was the sergeant who had asked whether an ambulance was needed. "Did you see—"

"Can't we look after Mr. Kennedy and worry about that afterward?"

Two or three people in the crowd called, "Hear, hear!"

The sergeant was a sensible man.

"Think you can walk upstairs, sir, or would you rather go home?" He bent down and helped Kennedy to his feet. The older man still seemed dazed and incapable of making a decision for himself. The sergeant, glancing round, caught Roger's eye, and Roger pointed upstairs. The sergeant didn't nod or speak to him, but went on, "Be better for you if you can rest right away, I should say. Let me help, sir."

Kennedy muttered, "I'm all right."

Eve went forward, and Roger pressed closer. The girl didn't speak. Roger followed the little group up the stairs. Eve didn't say a word which might be an attempt to tell Kennedy what had happened upstairs or what he was likely to see. Roger kept within earshot. The sergeant breathed much more heavily than the girl, and Kennedy's breathing was labored and noisy; Kennedy almost gave Roger the impression that he was putting on an act. Was that simply because he was prejudiced against the man?

There'd been little time to think, but sufficient to make sure of what passed between Kennedy and the girl. Roger had done that; now all he wanted to find out was whether Kennedy and the prisoner upstairs recognized each other. He mustn't forget that Kennedy had a tortuous mind. He mustn't forget, either, that the long arm of coincidence had an astonishing reach.

His arrival here, Kennedy's arrival, the shooting, and the man lurking in the flat—were all those things unconnected? He grinned at the thought; they were connected all right, the trouble would be finding out how.

At the top landing Kennedy stood without support. "I'll be all right."

He stepped forward.

"Jacob," began the girl.

"Oh, Mrs. Wedlake," said Roger, and made her glance round.

Kennedy stared—and recognized him. He raised his hands, and his lips parted. He was tall, powerfully built, and, usually, a strikingly handsome man. He was too pale and shaken now to look handsome, but was still striking. His iron-gray hair, waved back from a middle parting, was hardly disarranged. Although he moved with an effort, he couldn't conceal the latent power in his body.

He said, "Well, well!"

Then he turned and went into the flat, ignoring the note on the door. Roger put a hand on the girl's arm, then pushed past her. He was immediately behind Kennedy as Kennedy reached the door which led to the room where the constable and the prisoner were waiting. Roger saw him stretch out to open it, and stood so that he could see the man's expression.

Kennedy opened the door.

12

Humble Kennedy

The constable had done his job well. The prisoner sat in an easychair, opposite the door, placed so that the light fell on to his face; every feature showed up vividly. He was gripping the arms of his chair, and his lips were set in a thin line. Fear brushed his eyes, giving him an ugly look.

He raised one arm when he saw the others; he looked from Kennedy to Roger, and seemed to show no sign of recognizing Kennedy. The sergeant was out of sight, on the landing.

Kennedy drew back.

He was surprised; that was all. There was nothing to show that he was horrified or alarmed at the new development; it was simply surprise. He turned to Roger.

"One of your tricks?"

"Hardly," said Roger. "Know him?"

"I do not." Kennedy moved slowly toward a large armchair, and dropped into it. "West, don't worry me now. I—I've had a nasty turn. Please don't worry me now."

He was pleading, and making no bones about it; and he had been a man beset with pride. It had driven him to crime upon crime, had been at once the quality which had made and broken him. Now he was pleading.

"Please don't," said Eve. She hurried forward. "Jacob, hadn't you better lie down on my bed?"

"I'll be all right here, if they'll let me alone," Kennedy said. "I'd like a hot drink."

"I'll get it." Eve turned round, not fully recovered but in complete control of herself. "Mr. West, you can see that he's suffering from shock. Please—"

"I won't harass him," Roger promised.

The man who'd used the gas pistol sat through this, looking most of the time at Roger and the constable, showing no interest in Kennedy or the girl. The sergeant moved forward, and Roger put his head on one side, looked at the prisoner, and said abruptly: "Who sent you?"

The man tightened his lips.

"This is the second job you've done, and you can get seven years for it," Roger said. "Who sent you?"

The man didn't answer.

Roger turned to the sergeant.

"Take him to Cannon Row, charge him with common assault on Mrs. Eve Wedlake, and ask Mr. Sloan to see him, or let him stew until I come along."

"Very good, sir. Come on, you."

The sergeant took the prisoner's arm, and pulled.

A minute later the man was going downstairs, with the sergeant in front and a constable below. The gas pistol was on a small upright piano in one corner; Roger put the message beside it. The police were going to send a Yard squad in an hour's time; the hour would give Kennedy time to get over the worst of the shock—if it had really been a shock—and to be taken home.

His eyes were heavy and shadowed; he seemed a sick man. The glow of health which had been a feature of his appearance at his trial had gone completely. He was sallow, now, and thinner; if anything, that made him more strikingly impressive. His eyes were pale gray, he had long, thin hands and perfectly shaped nails; a diamond, set in a thick gold band, was on the little finger of his left hand.

Eve was still in the kitchenette.

Kennedy said, "Eve's told me what you think. You're quite wrong, West. The past seven years have taught me what a crazy fool I was. I wouldn't go back to jail for anything in the world." His voice was flat; that gave the words a strange emphasis. "The past is the past, and I'm finished with it—if they'll let me finish. They—won't. That's why I need your help. Has Lessing talked to you?"

"Yes."

The pale gray eyes were very steady.

"I didn't think I'd ever ask you for help. In the dock I hated you so much I could have killed you with my bare hands. That's all been drained out of me. It was seven years of hell, West. Not fire and brimstone, but gray, dull, deadly monotony; hell couldn't be worse. Take it from me, I'll never do anything that might send me back."

He stopped, and closed his eyes.

He was fifty-one; he looked nearer sixty. He looked tired out, too, and beneath it all there might be fear. He glanced up when he heard Eve coming, with cups rattling on a tray. She had made coffee; there were three cups. She put two heaped spoonfuls of sugar into one, stirred it vigorously, and handed it to Kennedy. He sat up, and she waited until she made sure that he could manage it by himself. Then she turned to Roger.

"A cup of coffee, Mr. West?"

"Thanks."

"Sugar?"

"A little, please."

Roger lit a cigarette and moved farther away, so that he could study Kennedy more dispassionately. The man seemed interested only in sipping his coffee, didn't look anywhere. The girl brought Roger a cup, went and sat down on the piano stool, and drank her own coffee. She'd tidied her hair, and her eyes were just normally bright; she'd recovered from the shock much better than Kennedy appeared to have done.

"What happened outside?" asked Roger.

Eve said: "I'd told Jacob that I'd talked to Mark Lessing. He thought there might be a message here, from you—he really wants your help. So I brought him round here." She glanced at Kennedy and didn't actually add anything, but looked as if she would like to say, "It's pathetic."

If his attitude were genuine, it was.

"Yes," said Roger.

"We were coming along the street when a car moved from the curb, behind us. As it drew level, the passenger next to the driver started shooting. He didn't hit me, but hit the car twice. I lost control, and we ran into that lamppost—I'd started to slow down, we weren't going at any speed, thank goodness. Another car was coming along, and a policeman commandeered it. I don't know whether the gunman was caught."

He hadn't been, or Roger would have heard by now.

"Know who it was?" Roger asked.

"I couldn't see the man or the driver properly. All I did see"—she hesitated—"was that he wore a bowler hat. It was a small car, an Austin, I think. Black."

"Thanks," said Roger. "Did you see anything, Mr. Kennedy?"

Kennedy finished his coffee, put the cup down, and leaned back. He took out his cigarette case, a slim one of gold, and selected a cigarette with great deliberation. He tapped it on his fingernail as he answered: "Only what Mrs. Wedlake saw. I did not notice what the man wore. West—"

He broke off.

"Go on," said Roger, and sounded amiable.

Kennedy said, "Oh, what's the use."

"You've queer ideas about policemen," Roger said mildly. "You broke the law, and the law caught and punished you. From now on, you're a citizen with full rights, so far as we're concerned. If you're being threatened or blackmailed, we'll help you as readily as we helped the people you defrauded before. If you're in danger, we'll give you protection. You ought to know that as well as I do. We're not vindictive. Maybe I don't like or trust you, but that doesn't mean I want to see you swindled or murdered. If you're really in trouble, why didn't you come to see us before?"

Kennedy said slowly, "Fine words. How many of them are true?"

"All. Try it."

Eve leaned forward on the stool.

"Jacob, I think he means that. Don't be obstinate any more." She sounded tense, anxious. "Clara wants you to tell the police everything, so does Charles. You might save yourself if you tell them everything. If you don't—"

She broke off.

Kennedy said abruptly, "All right! West, I am being driven crazy by a form of blackmail. Menaces, really. Men I don't know pretend to believe that I have a lot of money salted away—proceeds of some of my crimes, which you didn't find. It isn't true. I believe they think it is. They send me threatening letters, won't believe it when I tell their messengers I haven't any secret store. Ten days ago they started to threaten violence. They had me scared. After tonight I'm more scared than ever. They mean business all right. I don't know who's behind it, I can't give you any help but—I can't stand the strain any longer. I just can't stand it."

His voice, flat and lifeless, seemed like that of a man who was in the depths of despair.

Eve moved across, and stood by his side, so that she could look into Roger's face.

"It's all quite true," she said. "Surely what happened here at the flat—that message—shows you it is. They must have seen me meet Mr. Lessing, guessed what I was doing, and tried to frighten me off. They seem to be everywhere. Jacob's only told you part of it. They telephone at all hours of the day and night, send cryptic messages to hound him at the office, at home, and in the country. For two weeks he hasn't had a moment's peace. They demand—"

"A hundred thousand pounds!" Kennedy barked the words and thumped the arm of his chair, as if suddenly revitalized; thought of money might well have that effect on him. "A hundred thousand! If I sold everything I have, houses, business, my wife's jewelry, everything, I couldn't find half that amount. And listen, West, if I had it I wouldn't pay it. Be damned to them!" Color sprang to his cheeks and his eyes glittered. "I'll see them in hell, first. I—"

He stopped abruptly; there was a ring at the front-door bell, sharp and clear. He dropped his hands to the arms of the chair and gripped them tightly. He stared at the door; and if that were a true indication of the state of his nerves, he was in a bad way.

Eve hurried toward the door.

"Be careful, Eve!"

"I'll go," said Roger.

It was probably a man from the Yard; or the sergeant to report what had happened. He opened the door and stood back—and a little bundle of a woman came in, fluffy-haired, hatless, gray, with chubby cheeks and sparkling blue eyes. She wore a mink coat over a linen dress of pale yellow; they looked ridiculously incongruous. She pushed past Roger, and cried: "Eve, what's happened? Is Jacob here? The car downstairs, what happened?"

Eve appeared at the doorway. "Clara!"

"Eve, don't hold out on me. What's *happened*?" Clara Kennedy bundled her way past the girl. "Jake!" she cried, and rushed forward.

Kennedy was getting out of his chair. He tried to

smile, but the woman took his hands and drew him to her, peered up into his face and shook him.

"Jake, are you hurt? Are you all right? I've been terrified, ever since I heard of the accident, why didn't you telephone me? Eve!" She swung round, and went on in her rich contralto voice, "Why didn't *you* tell me what had happened, you might have known I was in *fits* of anxiety, it's too bad of you. Jake, my precious, don't stand up, sit down, you look so ill. Terribly ill. If only you'd told me earlier, I'd have been here before. Oh, Jake, what happened?"

Kennedy sat down, and she perched on the arm of his chair, like a fluffy hen. She had a small pointed nose, and her chin receded a little—whatever quality she possessed to keep Kennedy so loyal had always mystified Roger; it certainly wasn't her looks or her figure.

"Everything's all right," Kennedy said. His voice was stronger, and he seemed more himself, as if desperately anxious not to worry his wife. "How on earth did you hear about it?"

"Peter told me, he was coming round to see Eve, and saw what happened. He rushed off after those dreadful men, but lost them, and he telephoned me, from Putney or somewhere. He was so worried he hardly knew what to do. Eve—"

"I didn't call you because I didn't think you'd know," said Eve. "Neither of us was hurt, there wasn't any need to worry you."

"That's all very well," said Clara. "Are you *sure* you're all right, Jake? I thought I would find you at death's door, I did really. You mustn't stay here, I've told them to have your bed ready, the sooner you're tucked up in bed—"

She broke off, darted a swift, startled look at Roger, gulped, and stood up. She looked from Kennedy to Eve and then, almost furtively, back at Roger. She gave a little smile, almost a sickly grin, like a small child caught out in some trivial offence.

"Oh, dear," she said. "It's Superintendent West, isn't it? I was so worried I didn't notice you before. I'm sorry. I—I hope there isn't any trouble."

The richness of her voice faded, she sounded almost shrill.

"The police are going to help us, Clara," Kennedy said.

"Oh. Oh, that's wonderful!" Clara pressed her hands tightly together, and sat down abruptly. "So you've seen sense at last. That's wonderful. Have you told the Superintendent everything?"

She had a curious, childish charm; it would be wearing after a while, but it existed. She knew Roger's rank, but had always called him Superintendent. Her blue eyes were superb, fringed with lashes much darker than her hair.

"Everything," said Kennedy.

"Then you're a ruddy fool," said a man who stepped into the room. "You deserve all you get."

"Peter!" cried Clara Kennedy. "You don't know what you're saying."

13

Angry Son

Peter Kennedy was a younger edition of his father. He had the height, the figure, and the almost absurdly good looks. He was fair; his hair curled, the envy of many women, but there was nothing effeminate about him. He looked strong and rugged as he stood in the doorway, his pale gray eyes, the image of his father's, turned angrily toward the older man. He was dressed in a light gray suit which fitted perfectly; as he moved, it was easy to imagine the rippling of his muscles.

"You know what *I* think," he growled.

Kennedy said, "Yes, Peter, and I don't agree with you."

Peter swung round, on Eve.

"This is your doing. You'll live to regret it. I wouldn't trust West as far as I could see him. You don't know what swine these policemen can be." He ignored Roger, and went across to the girl. He gripped her arm. "I asked you not to do it. You knew I didn't approve. You've been at him for weeks, now you've ruined him."

"Don't be silly," Eve said impatiently.

"You'll find out who's the fool." Peter swung round to his mother. "You're as bad. In fact, you're worse. You know what he was like before, you know what prison did to him. Now you've brought in the swine who hounded him down."

"Now, Peter—"

"Don't 'now Peter' me! I'm sick of the whole crazy business. We could have handled this ourselves if you'd let Charles and me have our way. You'll find we'll have to handle it, anyhow."

"*Charles* wanted to tell the police," protested Clara mildly.

"Only because you talked him into it, you silly clucking old woman. You talked Eve into it, too. You—"

"That's enough," Kennedy said sharply. "Don't talk to your mother like that. If you can't be civil, go away."

Peter glared at him, but didn't speak. Kennedy's voice was much stronger, there was a note of authority in it which reminded Roger of the man that he had once been. He didn't get up, but seemed to know that his son would not defy him. Peter swung round, went across to Eve, and dropped onto a chair by her side; he didn't speak. He was a sullen, glowering giant.

All of them looked at Roger.

He said mildly, "How did you get in, Mr. Kennedy?"

"I walked."

"Doors get in the way, sometimes."

"I had a key."

Roger looked at Eve.

"Is that true?"

"Yes," said Eve, and left it at that.

"Why were you coming here just now?" asked Roger.

"None of your business."

"I'm making it mine."

"Listen," said Peter Kennedy heavily, "why don't you take a powder? Why don't you go away and leave us in peace? Go and control the traffic somewhere, it's about all you're fit for. Go back to the beat. Go anywhere, but clear out of here."

"Why were you coming here?" Roger asked, evenly.

"Go and take a jump at yourself."

"Peter—" began Clara, but stopped.

Her husband didn't interrupt; he seemed satisfied to let his son have his head with Roger. The events of the past ten minutes had stimulated him; he had a better color, and was sitting upright in the big chair.

Eve kept silent.

"I'm waiting," Roger said.

Peter sneered.

"Either you'll tell me why you decided to visit Mrs. Wedlake at this time, or you'll come along with me to the Yard and answer questions there," Roger said.

Peter flushed.

"Not on your life." He turned to Eve. "You see what he's like? Threats, threats, threats. From this moment on we shan't be able to call our souls our own. I come along to see you, and because I don't say why to the smooth Inspector West, he'll take me along to the Yard. Police—I hate the sight and sound of them!"

Roger said, "That's too bad. Why did you choose to come and see Mrs. Wedlake this evening?"

"Believe it or not, I like seeing her. I like her looks. I like her intelligence—it's gone wrong only about you." Peter stood up, came forward, and glowered. "Now you're giving yourself the right to inquire into our private lives, are you? Well, you'll ferret everything out, with your Yard rats, so I'll tell you. I'm going to *marry* Eve Wedlake. Any law against that? I'm in love with her. I'm not married already and I'm not certifiably insane, so there isn't a thing you can do about that." His face was very close to Roger's, red, angry. "And if you try, I'll break your bloody neck."

"Peter," sighed Clara.

Roger said, "I think Mrs. Wedlake will have more sense, but that's her affair. I—"

Peter aimed a blow at him; he expected it, swayed to one side, and the fist whistled past his ear. He sent a short-arm jab to Peter's stomach, and hit where it hurt. Peter bent double and staggered away, and Eve jumped up and hurried forward, as if to come between them.

Roger turned to Kennedy.

"Your son isn't going to be much help if he goes on like this," he said. "I'd try to find a way of controlling him. I'll do everything I can to help. Mr. Kennedy—" He turned to Peter. "Did you see the shooting outside?"

"Supposing I did?"

"Did you follow the car the man escaped in?"

Peter growled, "I suppose you know I did. Lost it in Fulham, caught up with another Austin Ten, and wasted my time. Now laugh."

Roger said, "Thank you. If I were you, I'd take

115

your father home now, my men will soon be here, to—"

Peter, still bending slightly and with his hand pressed against his stomach, gasped: "What? Why?"

"Someone broke in and attcked Mrs. Wedlake. I'm going to look for prints."

Peter straightened up with an effort.

"It's a damned lie. It's just an excuse to come and pry into her flat. I defy you to do it!"

Eve put a hand on his arm. "It isn't a lie, Peter, it happened. If Mr. West hadn't been here, I think I should probably have been hurt. He caught the man who did it, too. The police aren't the fools you seem to think they are." She turned to Roger. "Do you want me to go, too?"

"As you like."

"If you go, I'll stay. Someone has to keep an eye on them." Peter sneered, and rubbed his stomach gingerly. "Before you know where you are, they'll be planting evidence against you. Anyone who trusts the police is a damned fool, and won't be able to say I didn't tell them so."

Eve said, "Peter, take your mother and father home. I'll ring you as soon as the police have finished."

"Not on your life. I'm staying—"

He blustered on; it had no effect. Five minutes later he was helping his father down the stairs; that was odd, because Kennedy needed no help now; it was almost as if Peter were offering an olive branch by being oversolicitous. Clara clucked her way after them. Eve also went downstairs, leaving Roger alone in the room. He had seen

116

everything he wanted to see here, and went into the lounge hall.

A portable typewriter stood on the side of a writing table, on which was some writing paper.

The girl had left the door open. Roger closed it, went across, took the lid off the typewriter, slipped in a piece of paper, and struck each letter. The machine went smoothly and made little noise. He pulled the paper out, and put the lid back.

The girl was still downstairs; he heard the engine of the car start up, and knew she would almost certainly wait until it was out of sight.

He took the paper to the other room, remembered the door and opened it again, then studied the lettering. He didn't have to look far. The type size and shape were the same as those on the notes; and the *i* and *e* were slightly broken; not enough to notice, unless one studied it closely, but in exactly the same way as the letters had been broken on the other messages.

He tucked the paper away, and was standing with his back to the window when Eve returned.

She spoke at once, without a trace of embarrassment. Mark Lessing hadn't made a mistake. Trying to be dispassionate, Roger admitted that she and Peter Kennedy would make a perfect pair—to look at. The difference was that she had a mind, and used it; if Peter had one, he had never shown any evidence of wanting to use it, his manner was nearly always the same.

"I hope you won't let this make any difference to helping," she said. "Peter loses his temper too easily. He was deeply hurt when his father was sent to prison, he never believed in his guilt. He's vengeful, and—"

She caught her breath, as if that was the first time she had realized what she was saying; that she was pointing at Peter Kennedy as a suspect in the vendetta against West.

She turned away, and sat down without speaking.

Roger said gently, "Really fond of him?"

She looked straight at the window.

"I shouldn't like him to be hurt. I oughtn't to have said that. He's not the type to—" She broke off again, as if she realized that she was only making matters worse. "I don't believe that he would do anything like—throwing vitriol. Or paying anyone else to."

"Or sticking a notice on your door?"

"Of course not!" She flushed as she turned round. "It can't be Peter. It's unthinkable. He's such a boy."

"A grown-up, powerful boy."

"Yes, but—" She raised her hands. "You'll do everything you can to find out the truth, won't you?"

"I'll need to know a lot more than I do."

"I'll tell you everything I can, so will Jacob. There isn't really much more." She leaned back in her chair and looked across at a box of cigarettes, just out of reach. She didn't get up. "The main thing is that you've been officially consulted, and you know by what happened this evening that it isn't fancy."

"Oh, it's not fancy," Roger said. He took her a cigarette. "Does Charles Kennedy, the other son, have a key to this flat?"

"No."

"Someone got in here tonight. I can't see any

trace of a picklock being used, or the lock being forced."

He couldn't tell whether a picklock had been used without taking the lock to pieces, but there was no need to tell her that. He struck a match, and she took refuge in lighting her cigarette, as if gathering her thoughts.

She said, "I gave Peter a key last week. The threats named me, too. I didn't intend them to know about it, but he saw a threatening letter I'd received."

"Where is it?" asked Roger.

She took it from her handbag, and Roger read the short sentences; there was little doubt it had been typed on the same machine as the other notes—her machine. He put it in his pocket, and Eve went on: "Peter insisted on being able to get in and out whenever he wanted to, and—I gave way. He's very—masterful."

"Has anyone else a key?"

"Jacob has."

"Why?"

She didn't need telling of the implication that lurked in the question. She colored slightly, but her gaze was very direct. He could imagine a man like Peter Kennedy, strong-willed and tempestuous, completely losing his head over her. He could also believe that Jacob Kennedy would find her a refreshing, exciting contrast to Clara.

She said, "I am employed by Jacob Kennedy, and have a lot to do with the rest of his family. I trust each of them implicitly. Jacob has a key because it is convenient for him to come here sometimes, when I'm out of London. That is the only reason."

"Yes, of course," said Roger, smiled, and sat down. The squad was a long time coming, but he was glad rather than sorry. "Mrs. Wedlake, Peter's full of dangerous ideas. All I want to do is find out what's behind all this. That note on your door was typed with the same typewriter and on the same kind of envelope as one that was delivered at my house after the attack on me. That gives me a personal interest, not simply an official one."

"Then the same people are working against Jacob and against you."

"That's what it looks like."

"I see," said Eve, and her voice was soft, relaxed. "Don't misunderstand me, but I'm glad about that. If I had any doubt that you'd do everything you could, it's gone now. Please don't pay too much attention to Peter. He's all right, really."

"I'm not interested in Peter's tantrums," Roger said. He heard a car draw up outside, and stood up. "That'll be my men, I expect. Not that they'll be able to find much, even if the man with the gas pistol has left any traces."

Eve smiled; and he recalled how Mark had been impressed by the amusement which had shown so clearly in her eyes. He had the same impression as Mark; that she was laughing at him, without malice.

He didn't speak.

Eve said, "You've caught the man, so you'll hardly need to find out whether he left fingerprints. You just want to look round the flat. I suppose I can't blame you, and I really don't mind."

Roger grinned.

"It's normal routine, don't start looking on it the

same way as Peter would. We shan't be long. Are you going out again tonight?"

"I don't think so. I'm tired. I didn't enjoy being shot at. The only trouble is that Peter will almost certainly come round, and—" She broke off, and laughed. "He isn't the most restful company!"

"I can imagine that." Roger went to the door as he heard footsteps on the landing. Three Yard men stood outside when he opened the door, carrying all the equipment they would need: a camera, fingerprint equipment, and Roger's case of tools and oddments. Was it really superfluous?

He couldn't miss the chance of looking round.

"Tell me what room you want to look at first, and I'll leave you alone," said Eve.

"We shan't be long anywhere," said Roger. "We'll do this room first."

Eve went into the bedroom, and didn't close the door. Roger gave his men instructions in an undertone; they were to be as thorough as they could be in a limited time. The sergeant in charge said: "I get you, sir."

"Before you go, have a word with the woman on the right-hand ground-floor flat—right-hand coming in," Roger said.

"She doesn't approve of Mrs. Wedlake. Find out why, will you?"

"Yes." The sergeant grinned. "Maybe because she's a woman! I—" He broke off, the grin fading; as nearly as a big, heavily built man with a brick red face could look embarrassed, he did. "I must be crazy, sir! Mr. Sloan asked me to ask you to ring him, it's urgent."

"Right, thanks." Where another man would have rubbed the sergeant down for being late with the message, Roger nodded and went into the big room, telephoning the Yard while the sergeant passed on instructions to his men.

Sloan wasn't in his office; Roger held on while the girl on the exchange tried to find him. He was glad of a few minutes' respite. A dozen impressions had been forced into his mind, and the picture was blurred. Some features stood out clearly; the arrogance and bluster of Peter Kennedy and all it might hide; the most likely cause was good, old-fashioned fear. The fussy anxiety of Clara, and the tartness with which she had spoken to Eve. The Eve-Peter relationship; Eve hadn't talked of Peter as a woman would talk of her lover. The question mark suspended over Eve Wedlake's head was growing larger all the time. The keys—any one of the family could get in and out of this flat without much difficulty.

"Hallo, Roger!"

Sloan, on the line at last, was hearty.

"Hallo, Bill."

Sloan gave a little preliminary chuckle, which meant that he had good news.

"I've had a little chat with the man you sent over to Cannon Row. Name, Dibben. Employer—a certain Mr. Marino. Remember that Marino cropped up in this before, Bertie Downs was seen talking with him. How's that?"

"Not bad at all," said Roger softly.

"Not bad! It might break the case open. Want Marino picked up?"

Roger didn't answer at once.

14

Marino

The pause lasted for a long time. The Yard men were busy about the room, and the sergeant was careful to keep his gaze averted, but couldn't conceal the fact that he was listening. Cars passed outside. Once Eve Wedlake crossed the hall, to go into the kitchen; she stayed there.

"Still there, Roger?" Sloan was brisk.

"Yes. Thinking."

"Do you have to think? If we pick up Marino—"

"Leave him," said Roger. "We know where he is, don't we?"

"Oh, yes, we've kept tabs on him since we knew he might be concerned," Sloan said. "I'm not sure you're right. He's supposed to be tough, but if he really thinks we've got him, he'll probably soften up. I'd pull him in."

"Just watch him, for an hour or two, anyhow, I want to get some other things worked out."

"Please yourself." Sloan couldn't have made it more obvious that he thought these were wrong tactics. "How are things going with the lovely Eve?"

"How much do we really know about her?" asked Roger.

"Everything, of the last year. Before that, not much. She got a job with Kennedy's City company and was working there when he came out. Within a couple of months she was the general factotum. She's got her head screwed on the right way."

"I wouldn't argue about that," Roger said. "Dig deep. Find out if she knew any of the Kennedy family before she got that job. Find out how she got it. Find out where she lived and what she did before she turned up, and above all, find out if she was connected with the Kennedy family in any way before Kennedy was sent down."

"Right."

"Thanks."

"Pleasure!" Roger could imagine Sloan's broad grin. He knew exactly when it faded, too. "Roger, don't make a mistake over Marino, will you? Don't leave him too long. If he finds out that a man who knows him has been caught, he might take a run-out powder. Or else be given one. Remember what happened to Bertie Downs."

"That's what I'm remembering," said Roger. "It can't happen to Marino, can it? We'll be watching him too closely."

Sloan said in a more understanding voice, "I get you. If we allow time for someone to have a go at him, we can pick up Marino—plus any assailant."

"That's it," said Roger. "You haven't forgotten there was some shooting in Worrall Street this evening, have you?"

"No sign of the car, it got clean away," Sloan told

him. "There are thousands of those little cars, and you can bet it had false number plates. The bullets were brought in—.32's. Ballistics haven't seen any fired from the same gun."

"Oh, well," said Roger. "I'll be seeing you."

He rang off.

It was eight o'clock, and he was hungry; and Janet was expecting him. Janet would have to call on her reserves of patience a great deal while this case lasted. He thought of Snicker, and felt reassured. He went across to the sergeant, who was putting some papers back in a drawer, and said: "Telephone my wife, will you, and tell her I'll be late. Ask her to get in touch with Mr. Lessing, I'd like him to be at home when I get there, if he's free. She'll know what to do."

"Right, sir. I hope I didn't cause you any trouble?"

"Nothing serious." Roger smiled and went out, closing the door. He didn't hear the conversation in the big room when he'd gone; it didn't occur to him that a sergeant at the Yard would let himself say: "If they were all like Handsome West, we'd be okay."

Eve was sitting at a small table in the kitchenette, which was spick-and-span. Everything shone green and white. She was eating an omelette which looked fluffy light.

She smiled up. "Like a snack?"

"Another time, thanks. Isn't there any end to your achievements? Or did you study cooking in France?"

"Devon," she said.

"A pretty compliment to Devon," said Roger. "Good night."

"Good night."

He drove round the corner, saw a red *Doctor* sign, and pulled up outside it. The name on the brass plate was: Dr. Cyril Caslake, Physician and Surgeon. This was the doctor who had attended Kennedy. The whole of that shooting incident seemed peculiar: the timing, the apparent confirmation of the girl's story of Kennedy being threatened, and the poor marksmanship.

He rang the bell, and a trimly dressed maid answered.

"Is Dr. Caslake in?"

"He's still in the surgery, sir, he's had a terribly busy night. I don't know whether he can see anyone else, he—"

"Take in my card, will you?"

Roger gave her one. She glanced at it, then sharply up at him, and hurried away. He waited for two or three minutes, and she hurried back.

"If you'll just wait until he's finished with the present patient, sir, he'll see you. Will you come here?" She took him into a small room, where a gas fire burned low.

The youthful and brisk Dr. Caslake wore a white coat; he had the face of a professional boxer, and his nose was broken. His smile made him charming.

They shook hands.

"Didn't I see you this afternoon, Chief Inspector?"

"Yes."

"Have you caught the gunman?"

"Not yet," said Roger.

"I hope you don't think I can help. I was called

by one of the people who saw what happened, and wasn't anywhere near at the time of the shooting."

"You can help, all the same," said Roger, and took a cigarette which Caslake offered from a carved box of African teak. "What did you think of the man Kennedy?"

Caslake looked at him thoughtfully. "I don't quite understand you."

"Did he show the normal shock symptoms?"

"Yes," said Caslake slowly. "Yes, I think one could say that. Apparently he bumped his head on the side of the car, and that knocked him out. There was a nasty bruise there, but nothing really serious. When I reached him he was dazed and not very coherent."

"How quickly would you expect him to recover?"

Caslake chuckled.

"Your police surgeons will tell you that we can't be definite. One man might pull round in half an hour, and be outwardly normal. Another would be groggy for two or three days. As far as I could judge, there was nothing much the matter with Kennedy—but compare the way he reacted to the way the young woman with him reacted. She showed hardly any sign of shock. She may suffer a reaction later on, but I doubt it. My impression was that she is quite fit, whereas Kennedy is in a nervous condition. It's only an impression, and I wouldn't say it in a court, if you paid me!" Caslake chuckled again. "And you wouldn't pay me."

Roger smiled. "Well, it was worth trying, anyhow."

"Who is this Kennedy?" asked Caslake. "I'd a feeling that he was connected with some currency

fraud case, some years ago. The face was familiar
—have I guessed right?"

"A bull in one."

"If you really want to find out his physical and
nervous condition, get hold of a doctor who's examined him more thoroughly," said Caslake. "Mine
was only a superficial judgment, I was just making
sure there was nothing broken and no need for a
hospital." He put out his hand. "Sorry I can't stay,
I've half a dozen patients still waiting. They're
damning all doctors for keeping them waiting
while they lounge in front of the fire!"

He chuckled again, and showed Roger out.

Roger drove straight to Kennedy's flat, obtained
the threatening letters, and took them away. There
was no doubt they had been typed on Eve's machine. The paper was the same, too.

He went on to the Yard. Sloan was in Roger's
office, coat off, tie hanging loose, with a tray on the
desk—there were sandwiches and cocoa. He
pushed back his chair and raised his hands, as if
hopelessly.

"Spare a crumb," said Roger, and helped himself
to a sandwich. "What are you looking so miserable
about?"

"The Wedlake girl."

"Nothing?"

"She seems to have jumped out of the blue. I've
combed the reports we've had about her, and
there's no trace of what she was doing before she
got the job at Kennedy's office. She might not have
existed, for all we can tell. We'll find something
tomorrow, I suppose, but what annoys me is that I
didn't see it before. Mysterious people who sud-

denly appear like that are always worth attention. Kick me."

"I can't reach. Marino?"

"He's at the Three Bells, or he was half an hour ago. Drinking steadily, as he usually does. One of the Divisional men is outside the pub, with one of our boys. The Three Bells is only a step from his home. He hasn't had a message tonight, as far as we can find out, he's just behaving normally. There's one thing—"

"Yes?"

"Doc Gorley was there for half an hour, and left soon after Marino arrived. We've been inclined to rule Doc out."

"Have we?"

"Haven't you?"

"Not yet," said Roger. "The one thing we know for certain is that Eve Wedlake's typewriter is used for those messages, and that doesn't mean that they aren't typed by someone Doc knows."

Roger had another sandwich.

Sloan said slowly, "I don't get it. If you're sure about this typewriter, doesn't that make it pretty certain that the girl or someone connected with Kennedy is concerned?"

"Oh, yes."

"Then Doc—"

"How can we be sure that Doc Gorley isn't connected with the Kennedys?" asked Roger, and lifted the telephone. "Tell the canteen to send me up some sandwiches and cocoa, will you, and also tell them I'm hungry and I don't want fish paste."

"Yes, sir." The operator's voice held laughter.

"Thanks." Roger put down the receiver and pulled up a chair. Sloan was rubbing his chin, as if trying to see exactly what Roger was driving at; if his baffled expression was anything to go by, he hadn't yet succeeded. "Let's not start guessing yet, Bill. Just collect the facts, and when we've enough of them, start putting them together."

"I suppose you're right," Sloan conceded.

"And double the watch on Marino," Roger said mildly. "I take it we've a couple of men outside his house?"

"One back, one front. I don't think you need worry."

"I'd still double it," said Roger. "I should hate to lose Marino at this stage."

Sloan shrugged.

Marino was a barrel of a man with a rolling walk, who looked every inch a sailor. He was a dock laborer who seldom labored, and had never been on board a ship beyond the London Docks. He had a big square chin, unpleasant-looking little eyes, and nearly always needed a shave. His voice was hoarse and slightly nasal. He had never actually been in jail, and even the police wondered why. Balancing on the tightrope between the lawful and the illegal, he had lived for nearly fifty years.

Of late the local police had discovered that he was in the money. He said that he had picked three winners in a row, but no one was convinced, and no one knew the bookmaker. His money made no difference to his uncouth appearance or the fact that he seldom took a bath, and wore clothes which had been new a very long time ago. He drank a lot, mostly beer. He was married, but lived apart from his wife, in two rooms near the Three Bells. The public house was not far from the Mile

End Road, in one of the East End's mean little streets.

While Roger and Sloan were at the Yard, Marino hitched up his trousers, for he always wore a belt, and rolled out of the Three Bells, along the street, to his home. If he knew that he was followed, or that his house was watched, he showed no sign. He let himself in with a key, and went upstairs. His rooms were at the front, and the watching police saw the light go on in one room.

The windows were closed, but the curtains weren't drawn, so the light shone out into the street. Now and again the shadow of the man appeared against the window, but quickly disappeared. The watching detective at the front noted that the shadow did not appear after nine-thirty.

At ten the front door opened and a woman appeared. A street lamp shone onto her face, and showed that she looked scared. She turned and hurried along the street, and the Yard man followed her, until she reached Doc Gorley's house, ten minutes' walk away. She knocked, and the slattern who lived with Gorley answered the door. The exchange was brisk and brief; Doc wasn't in.

The woman from Marino's place hurried toward the main street, and the Yard man saw her going to a doctor's house; the lighted sign showed over the fanlight. She was admitted. The Yard man looked round, saw a telephone kiosk within sight of the house, and hurried across to it.

Roger West was soon on the line.

"Hope I've done right, sir," said the man. "The landlady at Marino's place has gone to a doctor. She tried Gorley first, and he wasn't in. I left the house unwatched, but—"

"You were quite right, but get back now," Roger said urgently. "I'll be along."

He reached the little street before the doctor. A scared girl admitted him, and didn't protest when he said that he wanted to see Marino. As he spoke, he heard groans coming from overhead. He ran upstairs, reached the tiny landing and saw the light under one door; all the rest of the top floor was in darkness. He thrust open the door and hurried in, with the girl just behind him.

Marino lay on the bed, gasping, his face a greenish gray, his eyes closed. Roger didn't think there was a chance that he would live.

He died before the doctor arrived.

"Arsenic, or I'm a Dutchman," said Roger into the telephone. "Bertie Downs died the same way." He was on the telephone, to Sloan. "I'm going to pick up Doc Gorley. The woman says that Gorley always treated Marino, he's treating a few others on the sly, and that's the charge we want. Is Peel on duty?"

"Just arrived."

"Send him over, will you?" asked Roger. "With all equipment for a search, I'm going through Gorley's place like a comb through a sheep dog. Oh, telephone Janet, say I'll be later than I thought, Mark had better go home and Janet to bed."

"Right." There was no "I told you so" from Sloan.

"I'll be seeing you."

Roger rang off, and joined the two detectives who had been watching Marino, and were now outside the telephone kiosk. He drove them to Doc

Gorley's place. The slattern opened the door, and whined that Doc wasn't in, he wouldn't be in until late. She also whined a protest when they said they were going to search, but didn't complain much when they were inside. One of the men went to put out a general call for Gorley, and while the man was gone Peel arrived.

They found no arsenic; no drugs; nothing to suggest that Gorley was up to his old tricks again.

Gorley wasn't found in London that night.

It was midnight when Roger reached the Yard, went up to his office, and found Sloan still at the desk. He looked sleepy, and was in the middle of another cup of cocoa.

"You'll turn brown if you drink any more of that stuff," Roger greeted. "Well, you were right."

"It could have turned out your way. I doubt if we could have stopped it happening, anyhow. Know how he took the stuff?" Sloan asked.

"We can't be sure. There was plenty of it, it wouldn't take long to act, according to the doctor. It was probably taken at the Three Bells, in his beer. The Division's looking after that. Gorley was close to him, although they didn't actually talk to each other—queer fact, when you realize that Doc was supposed to treat Marino if he had anything wrong with him. Gorley could have slipped the arsenic into his glass, so could half a dozen others. The Division's having a wonderful time, checking on everyone who was at the pub tonight."

"It'll keep them awake."

"Anything turned up here?"

"One or two things." Sloan was so casual that it suggested he had news that mattered; he didn't

133

give it at once. "Nothing was found at Eve Wedlake's flat, the only clue there is the typewriter. No
notepapers or envelopes like those used for the
notes, by the way."

Roger nodded.

"The sergeant had a word with the old buzzard
on the ground floor. Her dislike of the Wedlake girl
is based on outraged morals. Any young woman
who allows men to have a key to her flat, so that
they can go in and out as they like, must be bad.
She thinks Eve's a high-class tart. I don't think
there's much we can pick up there, Roger."

"No. Anything else?"

"Just a little thing," said Sloan, overdoing the
casualness. "I've picked up one interesting pointer
out of Eve Wedlake's past. Had a bright idea,"
added Sloan, leaning back and stretching, as if he
were almost too tired to go on. "I sent the descrip-
tion round the Yard, and of all people, Eddie Day
remembered her. Eddie was moaning because he
was working so late, but he remembered her all
right—not as Eve Wedlake, either."

Roger was patient.

"Oh?"

"She was known as Eve Banner, at the time.
Eddie had to look through some papers where
forgery was suspected, and she helped him. Her
boss had lodged a complaint, and—"

Roger said, "This is wonderful! Who was the
boss, or doesn't Eddie remember?"

Sloan's grin nearly split his face in two.

"Oh, yes, he remembers. So do I, and so will you.
Roger, our little Eve worked for the third suspect
in this case. She was in the office of the great Paul

Wiseman, before you and Mark sent him down. Isn't that fine? Now all three are involved—Kennedy, Gorley, and Wiseman. Going to have another chat with the luscious Eve?"

15

Job for Mark

Roger reached Bell Street at half-past one, and saw the light still on in the front room. A policeman on patrol duty was at the far end of the street, and Roger waited for him. There was nothing to report, except that Mr. Lessing had arrived just before nine o'clock, and hadn't left. Roger yawned as he opened the front door, and called: "Hallo, there."

No one answered.

He frowned as he went toward the front-room door. He opened it, and saw Mark sitting back in an armchair, one arm hanging down the side and fingers nearly touching the floor, hair drooping over his forehead, mouth slightly open. He was snoring faintly.

Janet wasn't there. There was no sign of Snicker.

Roger poured himself out a whisky and soda, and Mark didn't stir.

"Have a drink?" said Roger in a loud voice.

Mark started, his eyes flickered, his fingers

bunched; then he relaxed, but did not open his eyes wide.

"What's that?"

"Have a drink?" repeated Roger.

As he spoke he heard a different sound—a stealthy movement, not really like footsteps. He stiffened, and turned toward the door. Mark opened one eye, saw him staring, and sat up. Roger had left the door ajar, and it began to open; the handle didn't turn, the door just opened slowly and without a sound.

Then a nose appeared; a long black nose.

"Good dog," said Mark huskily.

Roger relaxed. "You had me scared, Snicker! Been upstairs, looking after the mistress?"

Snicker came in, allowed himself to be fondled, appeared to grin, and then went back upstairs. By then Mark was sitting upright, and stretching out his hand for the whisky bottle.

"He's been outside her door since she went up, just after eleven." Mark poured out. "Did you say something?"

"I wondered if you'd like a drink."

"Thanks, I'm doing fine," said Mark. "Yes, we did get your second message, but I thought I'd hang on. What's the time?" He looked at his wrist watch, and scowled. "Well, I've had forty winks, anyhow."

"And I can testify that you still snore." Roger sat on the piano stool and sipped his drink. "We're having a wonderful time."

He told Mark most of what had happened; everything that might be of real importance. Mark had a keen mind, trained as well as most men's at the Yard, better trained than some on scientific

137

and psychological aspects of criminology. It had always been worth while talking over a case with him. As he listened, his eyes grew brighter, most of his sleepiness vanished.

"So now all three of the beggars are involved," Roger said, and didn't seem to think that was amusing.

"Where's Wiseman?"

"Still in the South of France."

"Do you know what Eve did for him?"

"Only that she worked in his office and had access to confidential papers," Roger said. "There was a question of some share certificates that Wiseman discovered were forged. It was a year before the case against him broke, we thought he was honest enough then. If it weren't for Eddie Day's memory, we probably shouldn't know that she'd been connected with Wiseman. That makes her very important."

He looked at Mark owlishly.

"Why blame me?"

"I'm not blaming you. I'm relying on you."

Mark didn't speak.

"After all," said Roger, "you're a handsome man. Past the first bloom of youth, but Eve can't be far short of thirty. Peter Kennedy says that he's going to marry her, but I fancy she has some reservations about that, although she probably hasn't told him. I'd like to see what happens if Peter should find himself up against serious competition. It would serve two purposes," Roger went on seriously. "If you got friendly with her, really friendly, she might let out a few odds and ends that would be useful. And it would certainly make Peter lose his temper.

The more he does that, the more careless he'll become. Will you try?"

Mark said slowly, "She wouldn't fall for it."

"She might."

"She'd know that I was working for you, and would laugh at me from the beginning."

"That wouldn't do you any harm, and you might break down her resistance. If you pestered her enough you'd serve the second purpose, anyhow, and get Peter hotted up. I'm very interested in Peter Kennedy."

"I don't like it, Roger. I don't particularly want to be laughed at by Eve Wedlake, or Banner, or whatever her name is."

"Oh, it's Wedlake—we checked her marriage story. Sloan's been busy. When he knew that she was once a Miss Banner it was much easier. He hasn't got any farther back than the time she worked for Wiseman, but that's by the way—we'll find out plenty more tomorrow."

Mark shrugged. "I still don't want to be laughed at by Eve. Call me a fool. She's a nice girl."

He looked almost defiant.

"Like that, is it?" said Roger.

Mark got up slowly, and walked across to the window, then sat on the arm of a chair opposite Roger.

"It is not like that," he said emphatically. "I hardly know the girl. I do know that she has a way of looking through me, as if she knows exactly what I'm thinking. I get a sense of inferiority. I—oh, damn you," he growled. "I haven't really been able to get her out of my mind since lunch-time. Call me a fool again."

Roger said softly, "Bertie Downs and Marino

died. No loss, you might say. But that proves that whoever is behind this show won't stop at murder." He held out his right hand, and stared at the brownish scars. "In fact, he won't stop at anything. Not much in the way of serious attacks have been made on you or me or Janet, but they might come. It's easy to forget that this has all the hall-marks of a vendetta, and that it wouldn't be difficult for them to work on our nerves until we're at screaming pitch. Someone tore your books and had gas fired at you; next time they might try to kill. Eve's involved somewhere. We want to find out how. You can do that more easily than we can. You don't have to, but—"

"I surrender," interrupted Mark. "I'll play."

He didn't seem to rejoice over the prospect.

"Wakie, wakie," Janet called, and cups clattered on a tea tray. In the background Roger heard the boys, in the bathroom or their bedrooms. He opened his eyes and saw Janet, fully dressed, put-ting the tea tray down at the side of the bed.

" 'Morning," he grunted.

"What time did you get to bed?"

"Three-ish. It's not late, is it?"

"Eight o'clock," said Janet, "and I wouldn't have called you yet, but Chatworth was on the tele-phone ten minutes ago, and I promised you'd call him soon."

"What the heck does he want? Can't he sleep?" Roger sat up testily, and Janet sat on the edge of the bed, kissed him lightly on the forehead, and poured out tea. "Anything else?"

"The boys have been angels."

Roger grinned crookedly.

"That's a nice change, anyhow." He saw several letters on the tray. "Quite a post this morning."

"There's a letter from Margaret," said Janet. "Your sister only writes about twice a year, so she probably wants something. A note from the Joneses, about bridge, I expect, *that's* hopeless. Two or three bills, and this."

She handed him a typewritten letter, with a London postmark.

The type was much larger than that of the threatening notes, but the cream-laid envelope was the same. It was addressed to Chief Inspector West, and marked "Private" in the top left-hand corner. The *i* and *e* showed no defects.

Roger sipped his tea and opened the letter as Janet read the one from his sister.

There was a single sheet of the familiar cream-laid paper, folded twice, no address, no signature, and only a brief message:

Before this is over you are going to wish you'd never been a policeman.

Roger glanced sharply at Janet. She was chuckling as she read her letter.

"The girls are always talking about Scoopy and Richard," she said, "and Margaret wonders if we could have a holiday together this year."

Roger folded the message.

"What a hope!" He must have sounded natural, because Janet didn't look up. He tucked the message back into the envelope, said, "Nothing there, only a sales letter!" and got out of bed.

He was going to slip the letter into his dressing-gown pocket but decided that if Janet saw him she

141

would suspect that it was something he didn't want her to read. So he left it on the bed, and went along to the bathroom. He heard Janet going downstairs, and when he returned to the bedroom, the letter was lying just as he'd put it. The boys were already in the garden, and the sun was shining brightly; there was promise of another fine, warm day; they would probably have a bad summer when this spell broke.

He dialed the Assistant Commissioner's flat, in Victoria, not far from Mark's.

Chatworth answered himself.

"That you, Roger?...I have to be out of town today, won't be at the office, what's this about another murder?...Oh, I see. Think you're making any progress?...All right, do everything you can. Don't overwork, that's one of the things they're trying to do, get you worried and nervy....Yes, I know you had a holiday, you young rip."

He rang off.

Roger dressed and was finishing as Janet called: "Breakfast's ready."

The boys came rushing in from the garden, and Janet seemed brighter this morning; more naturally gay. Snicker sat in the doorway, watching them amiably; he looked incapable of becoming ferocious. Roger drove the boys to school, on the way to the Yard, and was there at half-past nine.

The office was empty.

A day without Chatworth to worry about would be welcome; Chatworth had a habit of descending like a tornado, especially when he could really be a nuisance. Roger went along to the large office where Chief Inspector Eddie Day and several other C.I.s worked, and found Eddie already at his desk.

142

He was a large man, very big round the waist, with tiny feet and a conical-shaped head; the general odd effect was accentuated by a pointed nose, a slanting forehead, and teeth which protruded slightly. No one who saw and heard Eddie Day for the first time would dream that he was a senior Yard officer; in fact he was brilliant at the investigation of all forms of forgery.

"Why, *h*allo, *H*andsome." A natural difficulty with his aitches made him emphasize them when he remembered them at all. "Thought you'd soon be around. Bit of luck, my remembering that girl, wasn't it?"

"Luck?" Roger knew Eddie well. "It was pretty smart, if you ask me."

"Well, that's nice of you, old boy," said Eddie smugly. "If I've got anything, it's a memory. Like the old elephant!" He laughed. "I've been thinking a lot about that girl, during the night. Stunner, she was—might not have remembered her so well if she hadn't been." He laughed again, for he was a simple soul. "I'll tell you what, *H*andsome, she was pretty good. One of the quickest minds I've come across. Didn't need telling anything twice, *h*ad everything at her finger tips. She seemed to do exactly what Wiseman wanted—that's what you're after, isn't it? *H*ow did she get on with Wiseman?"

"You don't miss much, Eddie."

"Oh, I know my job." Eddie beamed in the sunlight of this praise. "Well, she wasn't 'is secretary, as such. He 'ad two, and this girl helped them. She kept the records of the share certificates and did most of the work in connection with them. She knew every answer, I don't think she really needed to keep records, she *h*ad it all in 'er mind. She was that good. Wiseman didn't seem particularly friendly—cold fish, he always was. What I mean is, I don't think there was anything between them, *H*andsome."

"I wish we could be sure."

"Can't be," said Eddie, reasonably. "But I got the impression that he thought she was just another girl, and she might as well have been a machine, for all he cared."

"It's a great help, anyway."

"Just call on me when you want any more," said Eddie, and waved his arm, airily. " 'Ow's it going?" His aspirate vanished again.

"Slowly," said Roger. "Thanks a lot."

He went up to Fingerprints. A different man was on duty, and ran over the morning's message quickly; there were no prints, except those of a man on the envelope, which were dirty and almost certainly the postman's; there was only one set. The postmark didn't help.

Roger went back to his desk.

Chatworth, no fool, saw through the present situation clearly. "They" were out to unnerve their victim. It was cold war, played cleverly; and the other side had plenty up their sleeves. They were completely sure of themselves, and ruthless. What would they try next?

They?

Was there one, two, or three? Was it conceivable that Gorley, Kennedy, and Wiseman were working together? Roger wanted to reject the possibility as widly improbable, but couldn't. He was more edgy this morning than he had been for some time, certainly since the mastiff's attack on Richard. The letter had jabbed as a sword at an open wound.

He looked through the reports on his desk. A rushed post mortem confirmed that there was enough arsenic in Marino's body to have killed several men; that was the same as with Bertie Downs. Gorley hadn't yet been picked up, he hadn't been seen since he had left the Three Bells the previous evening. The police had last seen him turning a corner outside the pub.

Had he disappeared willingly?

Roger dug out the facts in various reports. The best was Sloan's; he must have worked for some time after Roger had left, to produce one which told everything he had yet discovered about Eve Wedlake, nee Banner. She was twenty-nine; she had married at twenty, and her husband had been killed a few months later. After that, she had resumed her maiden name for business. She had worked with Wiseman in one of his companies as a stenographer, and had left after his arrest, because the company had closed down. She had not worked again until she was engaged by Kennedy's company.

So far, Sloan did not know what she had been doing meanwhile, and had not traced any previous association with the Kennedy family.

The door opened and a constable brought in several letters. Roger glanced through them quickly; all but one were written by hand. The oddest people wrote to him at the Yard, letters from fools and fanatics came in by the dozen. Often they were anonymous; as often, signed with a fictitious name.

The typewritten letter had the name of a London newspaper printed on the envelope. It was not often anyone wrote to him from the Press; newspapermen preferred the telephone. He opened it with a paper knife.

He saw the flash and heard the sharp explosion, then felt his eyes burning. Pain seared through them and over his face and fingers. He crashed into a chair and sent it flying.

16

Blind?

Roger staggered against the wall. The legs of the chair poked into him, but he hardly noticed that. He was in agony. He heard another sound, a voice, and then felt hands gripping him. Someone called.

"Get an extinguisher."

There were thudding sounds, not footsteps; as if the papers on the desk were being beaten. He realized that, above the pain. It wasn't so acute as the vitriol pain, but his eyes were by far the worst; as if they had been filled with a million tiny specks of sand.

"All right, Roger." That was Sloan. "Come over here. Take it easy."

Roger let himself be led across the room and sat on a chair near the far desk. Men were running in and out; soon there was a hissing sound, and a foul smell; a chemical from the fire extinguisher. He tried to open his eyes and see; he could open them but could not see.

Sloan dabbed gently with a handkerchief.

"You're singed a bit, lost most of your eyebrows

and a few lashes, but it could be a lot worse," he said, and then spoke to someone else in a hoarse whisper, "Anyone gone for Mac?"

McKinley was a resident doctor at the Yard.

"Yes." That was Peel. "He'll soon be here."

"Not much damage, anyhow," a third man said. "The papers are scorched, that's all. Nothing's destroyed. How's Handsome?"

"He'll be all right."

McKinley, tall, plump, sandy-haired, came in bluffly, talked bluffly, seemed to poke his finger in Roger's eyes, and made the pain much worse. He was noncommittal; he always was.

"Get him along to the surgery," he said.

"I can walk." Roger felt annoyed that they thought he needed help, and angry with himself. He must be crazy; he ought to have opened every letter with care, both here and at home. At home. He stopped abruptly, and Sloan, with a hand on his arm, bumped into him. His voice grated. "Telephone Janet and Lessing. Tell them not to open letters—any letters."

"I'll do it," Peel said.

"Come on, Roger," urged Sloan.

Roger could walk; he wasn't really injured, just couldn't see. He remembered Mark telling him, comically, how he had blundered about in the room he thought he would know blindfolded. If anyone knew the Yard, Roger did; but without Sloan's guiding hand he would have lost his way a dozen times.

Three hours later, when they'd finished washing out his eyes, examining them and being soothing,

148

he was in a hospital ward again; blindfolded. They'd bandaged his eyes, and there wasn't a hope of seeing through the bandages; otherwise he would be able to see; of course he would be able to see.

Mark Lessing stood with his back to the fireplace in the front room at Bell Street. Janet was by the window, looking out, her face drained of color. Outside, in the front garden, Snicker stood peering through the open gate, and the boys were racing up and down the pavement, with Jonathan.

"Jan," Mark said, and stopped, then made himself go on. "It's no good talking a lot of blah. The big eye men say that they can't be sure for a day or two. Their first impression is that it will be temporary. It wasn't so much the flame as the tiny specks of dust that went into his eyes, they're not sure what the dust is, yet. Certain chemicals could do a lot more harm. If it's just dust, he'll be all right."

Janet didn't speak.

"The brutes haven't tried anything really serious yet—" Mark began.

"Don't talk nonsense, Mark," Janet said wearily. "They tried to blind him with the vitriol. If he hadn't been mopping his forehead with his handkerchief, they'd have succeeded. Now they've tried again. They've probably made sure."

"I know what you feel," said Mark. "You're bound to think like that, but I don't agree."

"How is he in himself?"

"Fine. Glum, but not hurt."

"Why can't I go and see him?"

149

"The doctors don't say you mustn't, they say it would be better if you didn't."

"I see." She turned from the window, went across to Roger's chair, and rested her hand on the back. It was worn slightly from the constant pressure of his head. She played with the material, letting it pass beneath her fingers. "I suppose they're right. They don't want a scene, they don't want me to upset him. I'll wait for a few hours, anyhow. If it will help."

She shivered.

Richard suddenly cried out, "No. No!"

There seemed to be terror in his voice, and Janet stiffened for a split second, then turned and ran toward the door. She was outside before Mark had reached the hall, racing toward the street. Richard was crying, Snicker was going forward.

"Richard, what is it? What is it?"

Mark reached the gate, and saw Richard lying on the ground, still screaming, Jonathan just inside his own gateway, and Scoopy, with his thumb in his mouth and his left hand at the hair at the side of his head, staring at Richard. Guiltily?

Janet picked Richard up. She looked—dreadful.

"Scoopy!" Her voice was strident. "What is it? Who did it?"

Scoopy looked frightened, glanced toward Mark as if seeking an ally, and took his hand from his hair but not from his mouth.

"I didn't—"

"Take your thumb out when you speak to me!" Janet screamed. "What happened?"

Scoopy snatched his thumb out, and went very white.

"I didn't mean it, we were racing, and Richard fell over my foot. I couldn't help—"

"You little *fool!*" Janet cried.

Her manner startled them all and silenced Richard. His knee was bleeding a little, and there were tears in his eyes. Janet put him down, turned, and ran into the house; already tears were streaming down her face, and her cheeks were as white as the paint at the windows. Snicker stood watching, and Scoopy came up to Mark and slid his hand into Mark's fingers. Richard came along on the other side, and Jonathan dared to venture farther onto the pavement.

"I didn't mean it," Scoopy insisted.

"I'm better now, if Mummy puts some cream on it," sniffed Richard.

"What's the *matter* with Mummy?" asked Scoopy timidly.

Mark said, "It's all right, old chap, don't worry. Remember your father was hurt a little while ago?"

"Yes, of course I do."

"Is he hurt *again?*" Richard asked quickly. "Is he in hospikal?"

"Hospital!" Scoopy corrected.

"Yes, I'm afraid so," Mark said. "I don't think he's very bad, but your mother's upset. Be good today, won't you?"

"I'll try," said Richard.

"Oh, I will," promised Scoopy eagerly. "I can be good, easily." His clear eyes were steady as he looked up at Mark.

"Are you sure Daddy isn't very badly hurt?"

"Pretty sure, old chap."

He knew that neither of them was really satisfied, but soon they were running up and down again, Richard with a bandage round his knee; it soon began to slip down. Janet was in the kitchen, washing up. Mark joined her and took the tea towel.

"Why aren't the boys at school?"

"It's a special holiday, or something, they're always having holidays," said Janet. "Too often." The tears had gone, and a little color was back. "I'm sorry about that scene, Mark. It's been getting worse. I tried not to worry Roger, but I knew that when the dog attacked Richard it was to do with this business. A woman at the next beach hut asked me what was in the letter Roger was reading, she said she saw him with it in his hand, and he looked so shocked. There was a mysterious letter this morning, too. He didn't say anything to me about it, either, but—I knew. My nerves couldn't stand that shock. I'll be all right now. I'll phone Roger's sister, she'll probably come and stay for a few days, that'll be a help."

"Good idea," Mark said, polishing a plate with unnecessary thoroughness. "I'll let you know what the latest medical report on Roger is, by lunchtime. Meanwhile—"

He smiled, almost self-consciously.

"Meanwhile, what?"

"I'll do everything I can."

"I know," said Janet. "Mark, tell me everything, won't you? Don't keep anything back. I don't blame Roger, but I must *know*, from now on. Not knowing is much worse than knowing. I shall start thinking that all kinds of little things are sinister —like that fall just now. I must *know*."

"I'll report," promised Mark.

He left a quarter of an hour later, and went straight to Scotland Yard. On the way he did a lot of thinking; it didn't get him anywhere. He went up to see Sloan, and Sloan telephoned Chatworth's office, then learned that he was out for the day.

"Anything I can do, Mark?"

"I just wanted to see how he was feeling about me."

"He'll use you and anyone else who might help. Think you can do anything with the Wedlake girl?"

"I can have a damned good try," Mark said. "Any news of my man with the bowler hat?"

"Nothing."

"I wish I knew why he turned up, just for that day," said Mark. "I wish I knew whether he managed to follow me all the time, and saw me with Eve Wedlake. If he didn't, how did these beggars know that I'd seen Eve?"

Sloan shrugged.

"Any news of Gorley?" asked Mark.

"Not a squeak of any kind. Take it from me, the only line we can follow is the Kennedy family and Eve Wedlake. We'll find what we want from there." Sloan was emphatic. "But be careful, they'll probably have another stab at you."

"I'll be careful," Mark said. "Any report on Eve this morning?"

"She went to the Kennedys' flat, just after ten o'clock. Peter and Charles went to the office, as usual, but Jacob stayed at home."

"Is the flat being watched?"

Sloan laughed gruffly.

"Take it from me, we shan't stop watching them until we've found who's behind this." He lit a cigarette. "Tell you what, you work with Peel. He's

153

dropping everying else to concentrate on this job, he's no fool, and he'll do anything for Roger. Why not have lunch with him, and talk the case over?"

Mark was enthusiastic—for more reasons than one. That meant that Sloan was tacitly agreeing that he should be kept fully informed of whatever developed on the case, whether Chatworth would approve or not.

Detective Sergeant Peel, fresh-faced as ever, his fair hair brushed down hard to try to get rid of the natural waves, looked youthfully mature as he sat opposite Mark at a chophouse in the city. He had eaten well, and now toyed with biscuits and cheese. They'd gone over the case from every angle, and there was little Mark didn't know.

Peel said, "There's just one other thing, Mr. Lessing, and—"

"Let's not be formal, we're going to see a lot of each other."

"Right, thanks." Peel was obviously pleased. "I know Sloan would probably laugh at this, you might for all I know. But there have been two attacks on Roger West. They were pretty well the same kind of attack, too—at his face. Or at his eyes. Anyone who throws vitriol is trying to disfigure or to blind. The stuff from that envelope was meant for the eyes, not much doubt about it. I'm wondering if someone has set out to blind Roger."

Mark said, "Could be."

"You don't think it's nonsense?" Peel was eager.

"His wife has the same kind of idea," said Mark slowly.

"The foul brutes."

"Know what I'd say, from that?"

154

"No. What?"

"Look for a woman," said Peel.

Eve Wedlake came out of Deverall Court, in Deverall Street, Mayfair, and turned right, toward
Berkeley Square. Mark Lessing, at the wheel of his
Jaguar, saw her come, remembered Peel's "Look
for a woman," and could not stop his heart from
beating faster. She wasn't ordinarily good to look
at, she was superb. She hadn't yet seen him,
wasn't conscious of being watched, and walked
quite naturally and quickly toward him. Her carriage had to be seen to be believed, and she was
perfectly dressed in a navy suit with white acces-
sories; everything was exactly right.

She drew level with the car.

"Care for tea?" asked Mark.

She started, and looked round at him. He
thought she was momentarily frightened. That impression soon faded, like the look of concentration
she had shown while coming along the street.

"Isn't it late for tea?"

"It's only five past five." He glanced at the big
square block of flats, fifty yards away. "Or have
you had tea there? If so, what about a little drink?
If it's too late for tea, it's early enough for a cocktail."

"I think I should prefer tea," said Eve.

"Wonderful!" Mark stretched across and opened
the door of the car. "Hop in."

She climbed in beside him, and he let in the
clutch and moved off. They ran into a stream of
traffic not far along. He took a narrow turning to
the left, several more turnings in the side streets of

155

Mayfair, where quietness reigned and it was hard to believe that they were in the heart of the city. He pulled up near a small shop outside which hung a sign with the one word: Lenora's.

"Know Lenora's?" he asked.

"Slightly. You seem to know every place worth visiting."

"Oh, yes, I'm worth knowing! I can pull strings all over the shop. Upstairs, I think. They have the nicest little chairs and it's quiet. No glare, no noise, and the best French pastries in London."

One of several little alcoves was free, upstairs, in a small and charming *salon*. Everyone they passed seemed to be talking in whispers, no one took any notice of them, except the dark-clad waitress who led them upstairs and sent another for their order. The china was delicate and pretty. The pastries seemed to be all that Mark had promised. There was no window in this alcove, and the walls were a soft, pale blue.

"What do you want to know today?" asked Eve.

"This is an errand of inquiry about your health."

"And Jacob's?" Eve smiled. "I'm fine, and he's not really ill. The attack shook him more than it did me, but he's been more worried than I have. He's much happier now that the police are really going to help."

"Wise man," said Mark lightly.

She started; it was only a slight movement, he would not have noticed it had he not been on the lookout. She glanced away from him quickly, but it seemed as if for a split second she had wondered whether he had used those words deliberately.

"Yes, isn't he?" she said. "The only one who's still angry is Peter."

"Peter hasn't much sense," observed Mark.

"Don't you think so?"

"If he had, he wouldn't have raged at Roger West as he did."

"So you really know everything."

"Oh, not quite. There are one or two odds and ends that I miss occasionally." Mark grinned. "Like more tea?"

"I'll pour out," she said. "I'm glad there's a tiny flaw in your perfection, Mark. If you hadn't told me, I shouldn't have seen it." Her eyes were mocking him as she poured out. "I'd hate to be disappointed in you."

"We must have an affinity, or something, I was thinking exactly the same of you," said Mark. "Contrary to the opinions of many people, I think you're a nice girl."

"Thank you, sir."

"And that Peter Kennedy is unworthy of you."

She handed him his cup, and laughed softly, took a pastry, and finished it before she made any comment; and he knew that for the second time he had said something which had made her stop to think.

"Peter is no fool," she said at last. "He has more qualities than you think. And you've more nerve than I expected."

She was mocking him again.

"Iron nerve, in fact," said Mark brightly. "What I was really asking, of course, was whether you're serious about marrying the man. I mean, there are limits to what I should do, aren't there?" He leaned forward, and for a moment drove the amused gleam out of her eyes. "Eve, I'm a friend of Roger West, and I'm interested in criminology, but

157

that doesn't stop me from being human. I'd like to know you much better than I do."

She looked at him through her lashes; that wasn't affectation.

"I wonder," she said at last.

"That's sober truth."

"I think at heart you're as much a policeman as Roger West," said Eve. "I don't think I like policemen very much. I have bad luck with them. I had a wonderful job with Paul Wiseman, and your Roger sent him to jail. Roger arrested Kennedy, and look what the years in prison did to him."

Mark took that in his stride.

"Why blame Roger?"

"Oh, I don't. It just builds up a prejudice."

"Break the prejudice down," urged Mark. "You may not realize it, but you're mixing with a nasty crowd. You may think Jacob is reformed, but even if he is, that doesn't go for the whole family or for their friends. You may find yourself in a bad jam, Eve. If you do, let me know. Please."

She wasn't smiling.

"All right," she said—and then laughter sprang to her aid again. "Now let's not be serious. What did you really come to see me about?"

"I've told you."

"I don't believe you, but it's nice to hear." Eve picked up her bag and gloves. "I must go, I have to meet Peter at half-past six, and I ought to change."

"May I run you to Worrall Street?"

"That's sweet of you."

They left Lenora's five minutes afterward, and turned toward the Jaguar, just outside. A man was standing against the wall, opposite the car; a beggar, dressed in rough clothes, carrying a tray on

158

which were a few boxes of matches and some shoelaces. He didn't move as they passed, and Mark didn't glance at the card on the man's tray, until he was at the wheel. Something caught his eye, and he turned—and saw a white stick, leaning against the wall by the man's side.

He read the card. It read: *Totally Blind—War Wound.*

Mark sat very still.

"What's the matter?" asked Eve.

"Eh? Oh, nothing."

Mark started off, but glanced round twice at the blind man, who didn't move and hadn't once called out, although he must have known they were there. Why had he been standing at that spot? It was not a busy thoroughfare: he could expect little in the way of gifts. A quarter of a mile away, in any direction, he could have taken a stand where thousands passed him. Why choose Lenora's?

They reached Worrall Street soon after six, and as the car pulled up outside Eve's house, Peter Kennedy strode forward.

17

Blind Man's Face

Peter's face was a dusky red, and his eyes were hostile. His hands were clenched; he took long, raking steps, and stood by the car, before Mark opened the door. He was as handsome as a Greek god and as angry as a man from Mars might be. His knuckles were white because he clenched his hands so tightly, and the look in his eyes didn't promise peace.

"What the hell are you doing with him?" he growled.

"Peter—" began Eve.

"What are you doing in *that* swine's car? You know who it is. Lessing. West's lap dog. He's several degrees lower than West, West *is* a policeman. That's what he calls himself, anyhow, Lessing calls himself a gentleman. He's just a—"

"Stop it, Peter!"

Eve's voice was sharp.

"Oh, let him drivel on," murmured Mark.

Peter said, "Don't ask for trouble, Lessing, or you'll get it. And keep away from Mrs. Wedlake.

Understand? I won't have you contaminating her. Just keep away."

"The complete master of all he surveys," observed Mark. "Mrs. Wedlake might have something to say about—"

"Not when she knows the truth about you."

Eve said, "Move back, Peter, I can't open the door."

He moved back, opening the door for her. She slid out of the car, and turned to look at Mark. She wasn't flushed, but there was a sparkle in her eyes, it was obvious that she was inwardly fuming.

"Thank you so much for the tea, Mark, and for bringing me home."

She turned, pushed past Peter, and went toward the front door; Peter turned and watched her, staggered by the "Mark." He actually repeated the name, in a whisper, as if he couldn't believe that she had used it.

Mark started the engine, and smiled up at him.

"Bad tactics," he said. "You're a fool."

Peter didn't speak, but glared round at him.

"And I think you're probably a dangerous fool," Mark said. "I'm in the middle of finding out. We'll have another talk, some day. Good night."

He drove off.

Peter didn't speak again, but turned toward the house. He didn't go in immediately; but Eve had gone in without shutting the door.

Mark saw Peter hesitating, and felt almost smug; trouble between Eve and Peter could only do good. He drove to the Eye Hospital, near Leicester Square, but wasn't thinking much about Roger. He was thinking a great deal about Eve. She hadn't believed him in his more serious mood, but he'd meant exactly what he'd said. That might prove to be a thing he'd regret. He wished he didn't feel as he did toward her, for she might be bad. If she were, she would be very bad.

He wasn't allowed to see Roger. That irritated him; there might be a good reason for it, but he couldn't understand what. He was told that there was no change in Roger's condition, that the bandages would have to stay on for several days and that when they were taken off, another examination might show a marked improvement. That wasn't much to take as news to Janet. He telephoned Sloan from a call box; nothing had happened on the case during the day, and Gorley was still missing.

As he left the call box and walked toward his car he passed a blind man standing at a busy spot with a tray of wares. That was normal enough, and it wasn't the same man; perhaps this fellow took the pitch because it was near the Eye Hospital; that would play on the emotions of visitors. It didn't play on Mark's. He drove at once to Chelsea; Janet would be expecting him, and he didn't want to get out of the difficulty by telephoning. If Roger's sister would come it would help a lot.

He could understand Janet's feelings; and share them.

He didn't go to Bell Street but to his flat, where he brooded over the situation and wished he were not emotionally involved. He felt sure that he would beat emotion, if necessary, but wouldn't enjoy doing it.

It was nearly dark when at last he turned into Bell Street. He passed a man walking slowly toward him, and thought that the light shone on a

162

white stick—a blind man's stick. It couldn't be! He pulled up and looked round, but the man had turned the corner. Janet would probably be upstairs in the bathroom, with the boys. He used his own key to let himself in, and found Snicker standing at the foot of the stairs; the one really good thing in this affair was Snicker. He heard the boys laughing; Richard had a gurgling laugh which reminded Mark of Eve.

Too many things reminded him of Eve.

He called out as he reached the landing, and the boys shouted a cheerful answer. Richard was standing naked by the side of the bath, pretending to help dry himself; Scoopy wore striped pajamas, and was drinking a mug of milk.

Janet's eyes turned toward Mark; and he hated the look in them. He knew that something else had happened, and couldn't guess what. She was forcing herself to be normal with the boys, who showed no sign that anything was the matter.

They were in bed twenty minutes later, talking to each other from their rooms, which were next door. In the same room they made too much noise. Janet and Mark went downstairs, Janet carrying the mugs and oddments from upstairs. She didn't speak until they reached the landing; then she turned and said with a catch in her breath: "Did you see him?"

"See who?"

"The blind man."

Mark felt as if the night had turned suddenly cold.

"Why—no." Even to himself that sounded like a lie. "Where?"

"Outside," Janet said. "He's passed several times

163

since you left. He's just walked up and down, calling at some houses, tapping his stick. It's been—dreadful. I—*listen!*"

They stood quite still in the dark hall, the only light coming from the landing. The front door was closed, but the windows on either side of it were open, and the sound came clearly, a slow, regular tapping.

Tap—tap—tap—tap—tap.

Janet gasped, "I can't stand it!"

Mark said, "Now, steady." He hadn't seen the watching policeman outside, but Peel had told him that Bell Street would be closely watched. He went to the front room and, without switching on the light, peered out into the street. Light from a street lamp showed a deserted patch of pavement. The *tap—tap—tap—tap* came slowly, as if the man were coming toward them; it was as loud now as when he had listened before, which meant that it was about the same distance from the house.

The blind man came in sight, walking slowly; it was possible to see his white stick. He didn't pause outside the house, but his stick rubbed against the gate, and when he'd passed he faltered a little. Then he went on:

Tap—tap—tap—tap.

Another man appeared, on the other side of the street; a policeman.

Janet was at the door of the front room.

"I think I'll see where that chap goes," Mark said. "It's a coincidence, but there's no reason why he should scare the wits out of you. You know you're being watched by the Divisional chaps, of course."

164

"Yes," said Janet. "Mark, I can't help it. It's getting me down. Come and stay here the night, will you? Margaret says she will come down tomorrow, I'll be all right when she's here."

"I'll be back by ten," Mark promised.

"You're so good," said Janet.

She went into the kitchen and switched on the light—and screamed! The mugs crashed to the floor.

The scream rang through the house, and set Mark's heart thumping as he raced toward the kitchen. Scoopy shouted from upstairs, but no one answered; he kept shouting, in panic. Snicker rushed toward the kitchen. Mark reached the door, where Janet stood with a hand at her mouth and her body rigid. The boys were running about upstairs; Scoopy, joining Richard, screaming, "Mummy, Mummy!" Richard began to cry.

"It's all right, boys!" called Mark desperately. "Mummy fell over a chair. She's all right."

That quietened them.

Janet hadn't moved; the mugs lay on the floor, smashed into tiny pieces.

The door was opposite the window. On the glass was stuck a picture—a man's face, with sightless eyes. A horrible face, contorted as if in terror, and with the eyes obviously sightless yet turned upward as if in supplication.

Janet fell back against Mark in a dead faint.

When he'd finished telephoning the Yard, Mark carried Janet upstairs and laid her on the bed; then went and soothed the boys. It wasn't going to be easy to keep them quiet, they were obviously

165

alarmed. Norah Thomas came in, and had a bright idea; that they should sleep in the same room that night. Scoopy and Richard held one end of Scoopy's bed, Mark the other, and they dragged it into Richard's room. They were soon settled, and talking brightly.

The front doorbell rang.

Norah Thomas appeared at the bedroom door.

"She'll be all right, but I think she ought to stay in bed. I don't think we need send for the doctor, she has some sleeping tablets here. I'll stay as long as necessary."

"You're a wonderful help," Mark said.

The front doorbell rang again.

"Forget it," said the neighbor, and went back into the bedroom, closing the door. Downstairs, Snicker was growling faintly, and his hackles were up. He let Mark pass him, but followed. Mark opened the door cautiously, and the light fell on Peel's face; there were two men behind Peel.

"All right, Snicker, friends," said Mark.

Snicker wasn't so sure, and growled when the men came in. Peel hesitated, then passed him; Snicker's growl sounded ferocious, but he didn't jump at anyone. They went into the kitchen, and then one of the men went outside, to try to take the picture off the glass. Mark who had already spoken to Peel on the telephone, went into more detail, and talked of the blind man who had walked up and down.

The Yard man came in, carrying a piece of paper, cut out to the size of a man's head. They examined the drawing beneath the bright kitchen light. It was cleverly done, drawn by someone who knew the job. The hair and cheeks and lips were colored with crayon; the piteous expression in the eyes was brilliantly done.

Peel looked up. "Now we know they're devils," he said thinly.

"We also know you're right about the blinding gambit," said Mark. "How did anyone get into the garden, with the Divisional men watching?"

"Someone fell down on his job," growled Peel. "I'll make sure he doesn't again. I'll go and see the constable outside, he may give us a line on the blind man, anyhow. You say you saw one, outside Lenora's?"

"Yes."

"Same man?"

"I couldn't be sure."

"We'll see if we can find this chap," said Peel. He went out.

Norah Thomas came downstairs, to make a cup of tea and some toast; Janet hadn't had supper yet, but didn't feel like eating. The other Yard men were going over the window and the garden, in the hope of finding foot- or fingerprints; Mark didn't know whether they had any luck, but doubted it.

Peel came back.

"The man was going from door to door, putting a Blind Aid Society envelope into each letterbox—it's a legal charity and there was nothing wrong in that. The constable noticed he went up and down several times, but didn't ask him why. He passed the house about half an hour ago, and then walked toward the Embankment. I think I can trace him, if he's an authorized collector for the Society. I'll have a damned good try, anyhow. As for the back garden—a man climbed over a garden wall, two houses along. The policeman at the back went to investigate, he wasn't gone two minutes—the man ran off. There was just time for an accomplice to come and gum that face on the window." He brooded for a few moments, then added, "Going to be here for the rest of the evening?"

"And night."

"Good man," said Peel.

His men had finished, and they went out together, taking the drawing with them. Mark went along to the kitchen, opened the door and switched on the light. It would have been impossible to miss the picture, and he could imagine just how it had affected Janet. It had been meant to terrify; it was both cunning and viciously cruel, and perhaps the worst part was that more would inevitably follow.

And Roger couldn't see.

The telephone bell rang. Mark went along to the front room, still thinking over the blind man's face and the devilishness of the trick. Why should anyone set out to *blind* Roger?

The ringing sound was sharp and regular; that of a call on the dial system. Mark tripped over the edge of a rug, saved himself, and snatched up the receiver.

"Hallo?" He didn't know who to expect and wanted to sit back and think.

"Is Mr. Lessing there, please?"

That was Eve's voice; he couldn't mistake it.

The voice came out of the blue, shattering Mark's gloom and simmering rage. He dropped into Roger's chair; and as he spoke, wondered how Eve had discovered where he was. That was a darkling thought.

"Speaking," he said slowly. "That wouldn't be Eve, would it?"

"Mark, can you come?"

She was abrupt.

"Why, what—"

"You told me to ask you if I needed help. Please come," she said. "I'm at the flat."

She gave him no time to say no, but rang off immediately. He sat with the receiver in his hand for several seconds. Her voice had been unmistakable; so had the edge of anxiety in it.

Had that been genuine?

Did she know why he was here, and was she deliberately taking him away from here; or trying to? Anyone who was waging this battle against the Wests would not want Janet to have company. He found himself arguing that out, while sitting and looking across at the piano. Janet and Norah Thomas were upstairs, there was no reason why he shouldn't go out for an hour.

He stood up.

There was a constable in the street, too; there was no need to worry about what would happen here, and he needn't stay away long. If there were any real trouble at Worrall Street, he could warn the Yard that he wouldn't be here until late, and the guard would be strengthened. He went to the foot of the stairs, and heard the two women talking in the bedroom. He didn't want to disturb them. He wrote a note and left it on the kitchen table, and went out to his car. The lights glowed, and suddenly were hidden; the policeman was passing.

"Going now, sir?"

"I'll be back. Be very watchful, won't you?"

"Don't you worry, sir, we're mad at ourselves as it is."

"Cheer up!"

Why had Eve sent for him? He would find out soon enough; would be able to tell if there were a genuine reason for the appeal. He had told her that he meant it when he offered to help; and he had. But doubt about her genuineness still tormented him.

She had worked for Wiseman and now worked for Kennedy. Why?

He swung into Worrall Street, headlamps blazing; they shone upon lampposts, dark windows, the pavement, and the fronts of houses; the street was deserted. No one was near Number 17. He pulled up outside, braking too hard, and looked up. Light shone from a window on the top floor; Roger had told him Eve's was the top-floor flat.

The front door was closed; he rang the bell just below Eve's card and stood back, lighting a cigarette. He didn't have to wait long. She came hurrying, and the pale light from the street lamps shone on her face, and her eyes seemed brilliant.

She drew him inside.

"Thank you, Mark."

That was both simple and effective. She led the way up the stairs without another word. The door of her flat was open, and the light seemed very bright. She looked pale beneath it. She didn't wait in the lounge hall and he didn't look round. She led him to the bedroom; the wardrobe door was open, that was all he noticed at first. She stood on the far side of the open door, and looked inside.

He followed her.

A man was doubled up at the foot of the ward-

170

robe, head thrust forward on to his knees, hands by his sides. He was dead; his head had been smashed in. There was a trail of blood on the wardrobe itself, and splashes on the clothes which hung above the body.

18

Third Dead Man

Eve said, "I opened the door, and there he was."

She swayed slightly, and Mark slid his arm round her waist, then made her turn away. He led her into the sitting room, and she sat on the couch, head back, eyes blank with shock. Finding the cocktail cabinet at the second attempt, he poured her a whisky, and took it to her. She drank without protest.

"I'm sorry," she said shakily. "I'll be all right, soon."

"You're all right now. How long ago did you find it?"

"I rang you right away."

"Does Jacob know, or any of the others?"

"Of course not."

"I wonder," said Mark, and she didn't make any comment. He helped himself to a drink; he needed it. He glanced at the open door, and a hundred questions flooded his mind, but he kept them back, and spoke flatly. "You know we can't keep the police out of this, don't you?"

172

"Oh, yes," she said. "Yes. I just felt that I couldn't tackle them myself. Even if Roger West came." She shivered. "You'd better call them."

He went toward the telephone. She shouldn't know that West had been injured; no one knew outside the Yard, as far as he was aware. If she really thought that Roger might come, it was a strong pointer to her innocence about the whole affair. He didn't dial immediately, but watched her; pallor took away little of her loveliness; her eyes were now too bright for that pale face, that was all. She looked as if she were fighting to regain her self-control, as if she knew that she would probably have to call on reserves of strength before this was over.

"Know the man?" Mark asked.

"No."

"Why didn't you go out, after all?"

"Peter and I had a row. He left in a beastly temper, and I stayed in. I wanted to put my suit away and change into a housecoat. I hadn't opened the door, until then."

She didn't add an unnecessary word, didn't try to explain what she had felt when she had seen the body.

"And Peter has a key," Mark said musingly.

He dialed Whitehall 1212, and heard the ringing sound.

Eve nodded.

"Do you know if Peter had been in the flat earlier?"

"No. Probably he had. I think he saw us coming along the street, recognized you, lost his head, and came running down. I don't know that, I'm only guessing."

A girl said, "Scotland Yard, can I help you?"

"Detective Inspector Sloan, please."

"Hold on, sir."

"Why not Roger West?" asked Eve.

"He's not on duty tonight."

She managed a faint smile; it was surprising how tired she looked.

"I thought he never slept!"

"He works too hard most of the time," said Mark, and then Sloan spoke. "Hallo, Bill. Can you come with a squad to Mrs. Wedlake's flat?...Murder.... No!" He sounded alarmed. "No, not Mrs. Wedlake, an unknown man....Right, thanks."

He put down the receiver, finished his drink, and pushed his hair back from his forehead. He didn't know that in a hawk-like way he was strikingly handsome. He went nearer the door, drawn as if by a magnet toward the room and the body, and he couldn't make up his mind what was best to say to Eve.

"Must you go in there?" she asked.

"For a quick look round. Eve, you know there's a chance that this was Peter, don't you?"

"I suppose so."

"Will it matter to you?"

"Up to a point," she said, and closed her eyes. "I'm not in love with Peter, if that's what you mean." She gave a tense little laugh; she was very badly shaken, Mark felt sure she wasn't acting. "I told him so tonight. I couldn't stand his aggressive domination any longer. I've stood it long enough. Mark, I want your help, and not only with this. I've tried to do a job on my own, and it's been too much for me. I may have tried too long, this may—" She stopped, and stood up abruptly, and he was surprised by the passion in her voice. "I'm losing my head! The police *couldn't* think I did this!"

Mark didn't answer.

She said, "Mark, I want to tell you everything before the police arrive. You can advise me whether I ought to tell them or not. You know that I was married. My husband was once very wealthy. He lost nearly every penny he had before he died. I've always believed that he died from being needlessly reckless because he was so bitterly hurt. I did all I could to tell him that money didn't matter—it *didn't* matter; I'd enough, and he—he would have succeeded, Mark, at whatever he'd tried to do. But losing it did something to him. He put it in the wrong stocks and shares. Oh, it was a legal loss, as far as it went, but he was badly advised. He was advised by two different people— Paul Wiseman and Jacob Kennedy. I always believed someone made a fortune out of Cliff, and that whoever it was killed him, by making him suicidally reckless. That's why I worked for Wiseman—I wanted to find out the truth. You can say it was folly, but I felt I had to know.

"Then Wiseman crashed, and Kennedy had already crashed, and I thought there was nothing more I could do.

"There wasn't at first. One of those silly things that happen started it again. I discovered by chance that Kennedy and Wiseman had worked a great deal together. It was a secret understanding, I didn't know of it when I worked for Wiseman. A year ago I met one of Kennedy's former secretaries, and we had dinner and she talked—and told me that. I knew then that the desire to find out

175

what had really happened to Cliff's money hadn't really gone. I just had to find out. So I got the job with Kennedy's company. Peter fell for me, and I didn't rebuff him—he might have been helpful. I wanted to know the whole truth. Then the craziest thing happened—"

She broke off, for a car drove along the street at a fast pace, and pulled up outside with a squeal of brakes; a second followed, and car doors slammed.

She went on quickly, "I started by believing everything that was bad of Jacob Kennedy—and now I'm prepared to believe everything that's good. He always swore that he was driven to what he did by blackmail, and—I believe him. I do, Mark. I can't understand it, but I believe that Kennedy was compelled to do what he did. These threats and the blackmailing aren't new—" She broke off, and then asked tensely, "Shall I tell the police?"

"Yes," Mark answered quietly. "Everything, freely. They won't let you down."

He hurried out and down the stairs, and opened the door to Sloan and the Yard men. Sloan came upstairs with him, while Mark explained what he had seen. He talked almost without thinking, was trying to decide whether Eve's story was true. If it were, it answered many questions, but—why had she started to investigate again, after a lapse of so many years?

She met the police at the door.

"Good evening, Mrs. Wedlake." Sloan was rather like a big boy on occasions like these, a fact which had fooled many crooks, who had behaved as if they had nothing to beat and soon found out their

176

mistake. "I'll see you in a minute, please. Where's the body, Mr. Lessing?"

He was formal now.

"In the bedroom."

"Show me, please."

Mark led the way, and a Yard man, a lean, dark-haired, and bright-eyed detective officer, stayed in the doorway. Eve was left in the big room. The bedroom door was still open, and now Mark saw what he had missed before. There were two or three smears of blood on a pale blue-and-white carpet and on the outside of the wardrobe, and some marks on the carpet, as if a man's heels had been dragged along it; such marks would have been made if the dead man had been dragged by the shoulders.

Sloan passed the open door, looked inside, and caught his breath.

"Yes, you know him," said Mark.

"I know him all right." Sloan's voice was harsh. "That's Doc Gorley. You helped to send him down once."

He was rubbing his big chin slowly. He had kept his voice low, it was unlikely that the girl had heard the name. He went across the room and closed the door, then turned back to Mark. "Why come here tonight?"

Mark told him; the story took some time.

Sloan pondered, and then said thoughtfully: "It could be true. If she was a spy in the Kennedy camp and one of the Kennedys is after you and Roger, this would fit in nicely. Put the woman under suspicion, make pretty sure that she didn't do any more spying, and turn the spotlight onto her." Mark had the impression that Sloan was saying this because he thought his hearer would like to hear it, not as if he meant it. He rubbed his chin so hard that it must have hurt. "Pity we can't call on Roger. So Peter Kennedy was around, and might have been up here and killed Gorley."

"Yes."

"What would Roger do?" asked Sloan. as if to himself, and suddenly grinned. "I can guess! He'd probably get you to have a go at Peter Kennedy first. No real reason why you shouldn't, and you might squeeze something out of him. Mind having a shot at him?"

Mark said slowly, "No. If you're serious."

"Take it from me I am!"

"All right," Mark said. "You won't forget what happened at Bell Street tonight, will you? I don't want to arrive there too late."

"The Division's looking after that," Sloan assured him.

Obviously he wanted a talk with Eve without Mark present. He couldn't get Mark out of the flat soon enough, although he tried not to show his impatience. His gaze was already roaming round the room, obviously looking for a weapon; none was lying about. Was that surprising?

Mark went to the other room, where the lean, dark-haired Yard man still stood in the doorway. Eve sat in an easychair, smoking. She looked up, eagerly, hopefully.

"I have to go," Mark said, and tried to sound natural. "I'll be back just as soon as I can. You can rely on Inspector Sloan—on all of them."

The eagerness faded from Eve's eyes.

"Of course," she said.

Downstairs, a wind cut along the street, and it

was really cold for the first time for weeks. Mark sat at the wheel of the Jaguar, lit a cigarette, and stared toward the street lamps farther along. Two uniformed men were outside the house and an elderly woman was talking to a gray-haired man by the door; she seemed to be outraged and angry. Her voice traveled to Mark, but he didn't take in what she said.

Janet needed him; Eve needed him. Or was he being a fool? He flung the cigarette out of the car, switched on, and started off; he crashed his gears. He drove straight to Deverall Mansions. Peter Kennedy lived there with his parents; so did Charles, the other son.

He hurried up the stairs; it wasn't worth using the lift, for the flat was on the first floor. He rang the bell, and asked himself what chance there was of finding Peter in.

Charles Kennedy opened the door.

He had his brother's height and figure, but not his looks. He was not ugly, but lacked the attractiveness of both his father and his brother. He was known to be much quieter, almost a retiring type, but with a sarcastic tongue. He did not appear to recognize Mark, as he said: "Good evening."

"Is Mr. Peter Kennedy in?"

"Yes."

"Ask him to see me, will you?" asked Mark, and started forward.

Charles did not need to pass on the message. A shadow appeared in the spacious, well-furnished hall, and Peter followed it. He was wearing a woolen dressing gown, which made him look huge. He smoked a pipe with a big bowl, and gripped it between his teeth as he spoke; it made the words seem like a sneer.

"Get out, Lessing."

"Stop being a fool, and—"

"Stand back, Charles," said Peter in an ugly voice. "I don't want to hit you by mistake. Lessing, you heard me the first time. Get out." He drew back his right arm, with the fist clenched; if he got a blow home, it would hurt. "Hurry," he growled.

Mark said, "You overgrown lout."

He didn't go backward, but forward. Peter loosed the blow, and it missed by inches. Mark closed with him, jabbed twice to the stomach and once to the chin. He took Peter so much by surprise that the man backed away, the pipe dropping from his lips; ash and hot tobacco spread over the carpet. Mark drew back as a powerful hand descended on his shoulder.

"That's enough," said Charles Kennedy.

Peter backed away, came up against a chair, steadied, and straightened up. He kept a hand at his stomach; Roger had hit him there only the previous night, but not quite so hard. He looked greenish gray about the lips, and his eyes were dulled, there was no fire in them now. He groped for the arm of the chair, dropped into it, and bent forward, grunting; the proper way to deal with that pain.

His brother closed the door.

"I suppose you have some reason for wanting to see him, or you wouldn't have come," said Charles comfortably. "Only don't try any more rough stuff, will you?"

"That's up to your brother. Anyone else at home?"

"No."

"What time did Peter get back?"

"You can ask him," said Charles.

"He won't be in a talkative mood for a few minutes, and this might be urgent," said Mark. "You don't have to be sensible, but it might help. What time did he get back?"

"Just after seven." Charles spoke quite calmly, showing no sign of losing his poise; he was probably used to his brother's outbursts. "What's so urgent about it?"

"How long was he at Eve's place?"

Peter looked up, and muttered almost incoherently: "Keep Eve out of it."

"I'd have a job to, she couldn't be in it any deeper."

Charles frowned, looking disturbed for the first time. Peter straightened up with another grunt, tried to rise but dropped back into his chair. The glitter came back to his eyes.

"What do you mean?"

"How long were you at her flat this evening?"

"Half an hour, but—"

"You were waiting in the flat before she came, were you?"

"I was. I shall be again. What the hell has it got to do with you?"

"I'm not worried about myself, I'm wondering what the police will say," said Mark.

Peter put his hands on the arms of his chair and stood up. It was an effort for him to stand upright, a greater effort for him to move; but he did. Charles stepped forward, as if to get between the two and make sure that there was no fighting. Peter seemed to sense that violence wouldn't get

181

him anywhere, and the aggressiveness was only in his voice.

"The police can't hurt Eve. What do you mean?"

"You ought to know," said Mark. "If you will leave a dead body in her wardrobe—"

He couldn't be sure; it was impossible to be sure; but the look of stupefaction on Peter's face almost convinced him that the news was a complete surprise. Charles backed a pace, and looked as astounded. Neither of the brothers moved for what seemed a long time.

Then Peter swung round and disappeared through an open doorway, conquering pain. Sounds followed as if he were moving about the room. Charles went slowly after him. Mark waited until Peter arrived in the doorway again, fully dressed. He didn't say a word, pushed past Mark, opened the door, and went out.

There was a faint note of humor in Charles's voice.

"He's going to tell the police what fools they are," he said. "Why did you come and warn him, Lessing? To see whether he would run away?"

Mark said, "Maybe he is running away."

"That's the one thing Peter will never do," said Charles. "Even when he should, he won't. He didn't kill anyone at Eve's flat, of course. He might lose his head and kill, but he wouldn't do anything to cause Eve trouble. I should have thought you would have known that ruled him out. I suppose you're sure the killer wasn't Eve?"

"Try that on Peter. Where is your father?"

"Out, playing bridge. He finds it soothing, I find it boring," said Charles. "I find a lot of things bor-

ing. How's your friend West? Does he enjoy being—"

Charles broke off and turned round; he had the
same easy grace as the other men of the family,
and was a much smoother customer than Peter,
probably much smoother than Jacob. "You might
as well come and have a drink," he said.

"Thanks." Mark followed him.

He ought to get back to Janet; he ought to see if
he could do anything more to help Eve. Instead, he
went into a large, luxuriously furnished room,
with a color scheme of green and gold, and
watched Charles Kennedy pouring out drinks. The
man's face was quite impassive, he showed no sign
that he knew he had broken off in the middle of a
question—and a question which might have been
significant.

Had he been going to ask how Roger enjoyed
being blind? If so, how did he know? For it was a
closely kept secret.

Mark spent a profitless twenty minutes at the
apartment, left Charles without having found any
other indication that he might know more than an
innocent man should, and drove to Worrall Street.
The police were still there; Sloan, who came down
almost as Mark reached the house, said that they
would stay in possession all night. He'd finished
questioning Eve for the time being; his men were
now listening in to the conversation between Eve
and Peter.

"Anything I can do?" Mark asked.

"I don't think so. We'll step up the pressure on
Peter, soon. If you mean, do I think it was the girl"
—he smiled faintly— "I shouldn't think so. She's

too clever to have let herself in for that. You'll be much more use at Bell Street than here, Mark."

"I suppose so. You might tell Mrs. Wedlake that I called, and will ring her in the morning."

"Right."

Mark drove off; and halfway to Bell Street he called himself a fool for having allowed Sloan to keep him out of the flat. There was no reason at all why he should have stayed away. Was there any good reason why he should have gone up? Peter would be booming and bellowing, and telling the police exactly what he thought of them—and Eve would be in no mood to talk.

Had she told him everything she knew?

He reached Bell Street, and found a constable stationed outside the Wests' house. There was a message from Peel; that he wouldn't be back tonight, and that he'd not been able to find out anything about the blind man, it would have to wait until morning.

"Thanks," Mark said.

Norah Thomas was inside, listening to Beethoven on the radio. Janet was asleep, she said, and would probably sleep through the night, she'd taken two veronal tablets. The boys hadn't made a sound....

They made plenty at seven o'clock next morning.

Mark, sleeping in the spare room with his door ajar and Snicker outside the door, woke gradually, and wondered what the unfamiliar noises were; he soon realized. The boys were rocking with laughter. He didn't go in to them, but put his head round Janet's door, which was also ajar. She was still asleep, but she stirred. He withdrew quickly, closed the door to shut out some of the sound from the boys' rooms, and went downstairs to put on the kettle. The newspapers were sticking through the letter box, and he pulled them out, yawning as he did so. There were three, and the *Daily Record* was uppermost. He glanced at the headlines, reaching the last one as he touched the kitchen door. Snicker was just behind him. He read:

C.I.D. CHIEF BLINDED
LETTER BOMB AT SCOTLAND YARD

He read it again. Snicker pushed past him, and stood by the locked back door, wagging his tail. Mark read it a third time, and skimmed the story; the paper knew everything that had happened, although the story hadn't been officially released.

Each newspaper had it.

19

Blanks

Janet was much better that morning. She laughed at Mark's efforts to help get the boys off to school, and watched him as he drove them away. When he returned, the daily woman was in the kitchen, and Snicker was upstairs, supervising bedmaking. The news from the hospital was "no change"; that was expected, and did nothing, outwardly, to depress Janet. She waved to Mark out of the front-bedroom window as he drove off, just after ten o'clock. He had talked a little about what had happened at Worrall Street, and she obviously knew his frame of mind about Eve Wedlake.

He went straight to Worrall Street. A policeman was patrolling up and down, and a dozen people were gaping—hardly enough to be called a crowd. A story of the murder here had been in all the newspapers, too; Eve's was now one of the best-known faces in London.

"Any of your people inside?" Mark asked the constable.

"Not this morning, sir."

"Mrs. Wedlake—"

"She's there, sir."

"Thanks. I'll go up."

The street door was open, as usual; although from now onward the elderly woman with the spiteful tongue would doubtless campaign to have it closed all day. Mark went up slowly, hardly knowing how to greet Eve—and the problem was solved when the flat door opened and she stood smiling in front of him.

"You're early," she said.

"I'm late. Hours late."

He took her hand.

"If you mean you couldn't get back last night, forget it," said Eve. She led the way into the lounge, and offered cigarettes. "I didn't expect the police would let you in, they were far too interested in Peter and me. But they couldn't have been more—kind." She used the word deliberately. "That man Sloan reminds me of a big puppy."

"Don't let Sloan fool you."

"I don't mean that I think he's brainless," said Eve. "Or that I wouldn't have preferred to deal with Roger West." She glanced at a newspaper open on a table. "How is he?"

"We don't know yet."

"You must feel—vicious."

"I do. So does his wife."

"Yes," said Eve, and turned to the window, looking out.

He could only see her profile, in all its perfection. She was frowning, and her lips were tightly set. He wished he could see into her mind, and guess what she was really thinking. The sight of her was almost hurtful.

She turned round.

"Mark, I do not believe that Jacob Kennedy had anything to do with this. I certainly don't think Peter did—or any of the family. I don't know what you and the police really think, but—couldn't this be a refinement of the blackmail against Jacob? These people who have been trying to frighten him might have found another way. Jacob is an obvious suspect for any attacks on West, because of his silly outburst in the dock. These people would know that. They could easily throw suspicion on him. They might turn round and say that they can 'prove' that he, or one of his family, killed the man —unless he pays them what they want." She came forward, looking earnest, almost pleading. "Isn't it possible? Isn't a thing like this *too obvious?* If Jacob Kennedy were really plotting revenge on Roger West and you, he'd be much more subtle. He would make sure that no one could possibly suspect him. As it is, suspicion is almost being thrown at him."

She paused, as if almost surprised by the heat of her own words.

Mark smiled faintly.

"Cause well pleaded. You could be right, too. Roger certainly considered the possibility. I'm not interested in the Kennedy family, I am interested in you."

"I *believe* in Jacob."

Mark said softly, "He could have fooled you, Eve."

She raised her hands. Her eyes were bright, and her eagerness put a new light in her eyes. She was wholly serious, there was no laughter, no half-mocking amusement now. She came close, and

Mark took her hands; she was standing, he was sitting.

"I don't think he has, Mark."

"All right—what about Peter?"

"Oh, *Peter* didn't kill the man who was found here last night. I wouldn't put it past him to attack Roger West, he's passionately devoted to his father and hates the sight and sound of a policeman, but it would be an open attack. He'd start a fracas in the street, or something like that. He isn't the type to do things by stealth, and employ others to do his dirty work for him. It's no use trying to say that he might have done it, Mark—people don't act out of character as wildly as that. Now if Charles were the suspect—"

She paused.

"So you don't like Charles."

"He's the only member of the family whom I don't trust," Eve said quietly. "It's hard to say why. He keeps very quiet, he's always at hand, he thinks a lot and seldom says what he thinks. He has a good mind. He pretends that he hasn't any physical courage, but I'm not sure. I think he's by far the cleverest member of the family, with a mind which might be warped enough to plan a campaign like this—except for one thing."

"What's that?"

"Devotion to his father." Eve didn't pull her hands free, but stood looking down; and because of the distraction of her beauty it was hard to concentrate on what she was saying. It was breathless beauty—real and natural, although it seemed so near perfection. "Mark, listen to me. You've the ear of the police, and they must know these things. That family is absolutely devoted, one to another.

I've never come across anything quite like it. They work together, play together, plan together. They've a loyalty to each other which you have to live with to believe. They bicker a bit among themselves sometimes, but much less than most families. I've known them for a long time now, and I've never heard Jacob and Clara have a cross word. There's a bond of love there which is unbreakable and—almost unique. I don't think it's a bond that would exist if there were real badness in them, but if one of the family is seeking vengeance for what happened to Jacob, I think it's Charles."

She pulled her hands free, backed away, and forced a laugh. That didn't sound natural, because she wasn't amused.

"I'm sorry I'm so vehement."

"Don't be sorry," Mark said softly, and stood up. "What happened to Peter last night?"

"He went away with Sloan, and I think they questioned him at Scotland Yard, but he's back at the flat now—or rather at the office. All the men went in together this morning, Clara rang me up to say so."

"No arrest," murmured Mark.

"Not of a Kennedy."

"Well, it's something, if only negative." Mark took her hands again. "Eve, I don't know the truth, I can't see through the fog. I only wish you were out of it, because I think there's danger—and you know there is." She didn't deny that; she didn't take her hands away. "Is there anything you haven't told me?"

"Nothing."

"If you learn anything else, will you tell me?"

"Yes."

"Even if it means betraying a Kennedy?"

"I like them," Eve said quietly. "I'm fond of them. But if they're behind this, then I'll help to catch them. I'd heard of West and of you before, of course, but you were just names. You're much more than a name now. And you seem to forget that there's as much danger for you as for Roger West. Be careful, Mark."

"I'll be careful," he said.

Quite suddenly, on an impulse too strong to reject, he pulled her close and kissed her. He felt the warm pressure of her lips and of her body. He felt the hint of passion, too, and believed in a wild moment of ecstasy that she felt as much as he—that he mattered to her.

He stood back, and she was breathless. He squeezed her hand and turned away.

When he reached the street she was looking at him out of the window.

Sloan was alone in Roger's office at the Yard. He glanced up when he saw Mark, waved, pointed to a chair, and went on with what he was reading. Mark sat back in an easychair, smoked, tried to think of the things that ought to be on his mind, and saw mind-pictures of Eve appearing everywhere; even in the front of Sloan's fair head.

Sloan looked up, and pushed the papers aside.

"Sorry. How are tricks?"

"Not too bad. Janet's much better."

"Ugly business," Sloan said heavily. "I wish to heaven we were nearer the end of it. We've found a few odds and ends, but nothing much, except one thing. Gorley arrived at Worrall Street about five o'clock yesterday afternoon, and appears to have

191

let himself in with a key. So many people have keys to that flat, it isn't surprising. It's pretty certain that he went there by appointment. Another man arrived by car and went in at half-past five. He left alone twenty minutes later. Gorley wasn't seen to leave. We picked all this up from neighbors, of course, not all from the same neighbor."

Mark nodded.

"The little man who was there for twenty minutes, and who could have killed Gorley, wore a dark suit and a bowler hat," said Sloan.

"So he's popped up again."

"His car hasn't. There's another thing, too. Peter Kennedy arrived soon after the little man. There was a regular procession of them there yesterday —much to the disgust of one of the tenants downstairs." Sloan smiled faintly. "That wasn't unusual. Kennedy often saw people at Eve Wedlake's flat, if he didn't want to interview them at his office or at Deverall Court. His reason's plausible enough—he preferred not to let everyone with whom he did business know that he was Jacob Kennedy, the man who spent so long in jail. We've ample evidence that he was often at the flat when there were callers. It was used as a kind of subsidiary office."

"I see," said Mark heavily.

"The time of the murder was between four and seven o'clock, according to the police surgeon— and that fits in with what we know. The only one of the Kennedy family who can't produce corroboration to say where he was between those hours is Peter—we've only his word for it, and the neighbors' statements covering part of the time. The other Kennedys were miles away." Sloan was talking quickly, as if he were reciting a well-learned lesson. "It's fairly clear that Gorley had an appointment with someone there and that the someone was the little man. It's also fairly clear that we should be expected to take it for granted that one of the Kennedy family made that appointment. Gorley waited—and was killed. We can guess why. He could have told us more than Bertie Downs and more than even Marino, and his killer made sure that he couldn't talk. Be very careful, Mark."

"I'll be careful."

"And don't let anyone fool you."

Mark smiled. "Eve Wedlake was with me until she got back to her flat. She couldn't—"

"Oh, yes, she could," said Sloan. "Don't make any mistake, she could have killed him. Look at the facts. The little man with the bowler hat came and went in twenty minutes—if Gorley had hidden in the wardrobe the man might never have seen him. Eve Wedlake had a row with Peter, and sent him packing. That left her alone in the flat, until she telephoned you and told you what she'd discovered."

Mark sat very still, not liking this.

"Just imagine that she went into her bedroom and discovered that Gorley was there, lying in wait for her. And supposing she had reason to fear Gorley. What would be easier than for her to come out of the bedroom, stage the row with Peter, make sure he'd gone, and then come back and deal with Gorley? The blows on the back of the head could have been struck by a woman, we've established that."

Mark said, "Why haven't you charged her?"

"Oh, come! We want some direct evidence, all we

193

have yet is circumstantial. She won't be left alone until we can be pretty sure she didn't do it. Sorry," Sloan added. "Better to be blunt, isn't it?"

"Yes. Thanks."

The telephone bell rang.

"Excuse me," said Sloan, and took it off the receiver.

He didn't appear to be looking at Mark, but actually watched him covertly. Mark sat back in his chair, eyes narrowed, expression quite blank. Practically everything that Sloan had said about Eve had hit him like a blow from a hammer; and the blows still hurt. He couldn't argue with the logic of it; Sloan might be right. Something in him went farther; that Sloan was probably right.

The little man in the bowler hat had watched him one morning—the very morning on which Eve had chosen to talk to him. She'd forced that meeting, she'd wanted it. Why?

Sloan kept saying, "Yes," and the man at the other end of the line seemed to talk for a long time.

At last, Sloan said, "If he will, yes. Don't wait more than three-quarters of an hour. 'By." He rang off, and looked straight at Mark. "That was Peel, and he's traced the blind man who walked up and down Bell Street last night. Would you like to be there when he talks to him?"

Mark jumped up, suddenly eager.

"Where are they?" he demanded.

The blind man was of medium build, but frail and old. He lived in a single furnished room on the ground floor of a big, terraced house in Bloomsbury. His name was Kaye—William Kaye. He had been blinded in the First World War, and he was employed, as so many others like him, in the annual collection for the Blind Aid Society, because he had taught himself to move about so freely.

He had been stopped when delivering his envelopes in Fulham, on the Chelsea side of the borough. He had been asked to work in Bell Street, and to walk up and down several times, and had believed it when he had been told that if he did so he would probably get extremely good results from the collection envelopes. He had also been specially asked to walk there at dusk—and for his trouble he had been given a donation of five pounds.

He had not been able to see the person who had talked to him, of course. All he knew was that it was a young woman, who had pulled up near him in a car.

No one had seen the encounter between blind William Kaye and the unnamed woman. A second blind man was found, who had been asked to stay outside Lenora's; and anyone could easily find out that Mark Lessing went there frequently. A woman had also spoken to him, using the same arguments and giving the same bribe. The pound notes were examined; none of them carried helpful fingerprints.

The trail petered out.

Peel followed it for several days, sometimes with Mark, sometimes on his own. He also followed the trail of Gorley's movements, but learned nothing more. Nothing else came to light about the Kennedys or Eve Wedlake. After consultations with Chatworth, Sloan held his hand. Eve went to the office or to Kennedy's flat, as usual—the only change was that the Worrall Street flat was no longer used for appointments. The quarrel between Peter and Eve was patched up; according to Eve, Peter wasn't quite the same. The Kennedys' business was legitimate; there was no reason at all to suspect anything criminal in it. No further threats were received by Kennedy or members of his family during those few days; there were no further incidents at Bell Street or at Mark's flat.

Everything led to a dead end.

On the fifth day the bandages were to be taken off Roger's eyes.

20

Bright Morning

Roger sat in an easychair in the small ward at the hospital, fully dressed, except that he had on no collar and tie, and wore slippers. Janet had brought the slippers and other things he had needed, when the doctors had said that it would be safe for her to see him.

Roger was going over that meeting now.

Janet had said little that really mattered; nothing of her feelings. He'd known all about those, however, from the very tone of her voice. His sister was at Bell Street, Mark was wonderful, Snicker was too good to be believed, there'd been no trouble of any kind.

Roger had known agony, because he hadn't been able to see her.

She'd talked almost lightly, as if it were only a matter of a few days before he could see properly again, and there was no risk that the injury would be permanent; and she'd left, after three-quarters of an hour, telling him a parting story of one of the latest antics of the boys.

She'd been in each day since.

She knew that the bandages were to be removed today.

He leaned back, smoking a cigarette which the nurse had lit for him a few minutes earlier. An ashtray was within reach, on a table by his side. So were cigarettes and matches if he chose to try to light one himself. He knew the position of the case; Sloan, Peel, and Mark had each been in several times. He'd checked what one told him against another's story, clarified certain details, felt sure that nothing of consequence had been kept from him. He forced himself to put all the facts in their proper perspective, examined them dispassionately from time to time, and came to the same conclusion as Peel and Janet—that someone was deliberately setting out to blind him.

What greater revenge could there be than that?

The doctors and the surgeon were due at noon; the nurse had told him that it was twenty minutes to twelve; nearly ten must have passed, he could feel the warmth of the cigarette at his lips when he drew on it; that meant that it was nearly finished. He stubbed it out in the ashtray, cautiously, then squared his shoulders and told himself that only a fool would refuse to face the facts.

He was probably blind.

The doctors had been frank, knowing that it was the wisest course. The explosive envelope had contained finely powdered glass mixed together with a chemical which, if it had affected the optic nerves, could blind him for life. There was no way of telling how much of the treated glass had actually got into the eye. They had been able to ease most of the pain; his eyes hurt, at times, but never agonizingly; there was no indication of the future from that, the only indication would be from another examination—today.

He heard footsteps outside; men's footsteps.

A doctor and a surgeon entered.

He could see. The room was darkened, yet what little light there was hurt his eyes; but he could see.

"You're going to be all right, Mr. West," said the surgeon, Brailsford, a tall and pale man with a prominent nose and eyes which looked too weak to examine those of other people. "You'll have a lot of discomfort for a while, and I shouldn't use your eyes much for the next few weeks. Say a month. Don't read anything in small print, don't go to the films or the theater, if you go for a car ride wear dark glasses. Always wear dark glasses in sunlight —otherwise you'll retard your progress. You needn't worry beyond that."

Mark opened the door of the Bell Street house. Janet, with a hand on Roger's arm, helped him over the threshold.

It was two days after the specialist's verdict. Roger wore dark glasses, and there were times when his eyes hurt so much that he thought the great man might have been wrong. At others he could see much more clearly. He let Janet lead him across the room, toward his own armchair. Snicker was fussing about his knees. It was twelve-thirty; the boys would be home for lunch in a quarter of an hour.

The short car ride from Leicester Square had tired Roger, he was glad to sit down and relax.

"If I go on at this rate," he said, "I'll be pensioned off on half-pay before long."

"If they'd pension you on quarter-pay I'd be happy," said Janet. "*I* could work, and you could do the home chores, darling. I'd feel much safer."

"Yes, dear."

"Anyone like a drink?" asked Mark.

"Not a bad idea," said Roger. "Gin, I think, with a splash of orange—unless some bright spark thought of champagne."

"I'm your champagne."

Janet rested a hand on his shoulder, and he could tell that her voice reflected the easing of suspense and uncertainty. Over a week had passed, nothing had happened, the lull might be more than a lull. His own relief was still predominant; he would soon be able to see as well as the next man, and nothing else greatly mattered.

He heard Mark pouring out the drinks, then heard footsteps on the path.

"Postman," said Janet. "I'll get it."

She hurried out, talked cheerfully to the postman, and then suddenly stopped speaking. The postman started on his way back to the gate. There was no sound from Janet, she neither spoke nor moved. Roger felt tension rising. He turned his head, and through the dark lenses just saw Mark staring toward the open door. Mark moved toward it, darting him a look which he obviously hoped Roger would not see.

Janet and Mark met at the door.

Roger said harshly, "Don't open it yet!"

"I'll open it carefully," Mark said. He held the

letter to one side; nothing happened as he took out the paper. Janet and he read it together.

Roger's voice was husky.

"What is it? Don't hold out on me."

Janet cleared her throat; paper rustled, and Roger saw the letter in her hand. Mark put an arm round Janet's waist. Roger couldn't see her face properly, but knew from that sign that she was suffering from shock; fierce, hurtful shock.

"What is it?"

Mark said, "Another letter. Typewritten. On the typewriter with the big print. It says—" He paused, and the period of waiting seemed endless. "It says, *'What a funny thing happened at school this morning. It's hardly started yet.'*"

After a second's pause Roger shouted, "Get to the school, don't stand there. Get to the school!"

The two hundred and twenty-seven pupils at the nearby school who had free milk in the mornings were ill that lunchtime and afternoon. Many were taken to hospital, most treated at home; Richard and Scoopy were treated at home. They were violently sick, their temperatures rocketed, and they were in some pain; at least the doctor was able to ease that for them.

The milk was delivered to the school in a sealed container from the dairy, and handed out to the children in cups. It had a solution of arsenic mixed with it.

There were no fatalities.

"How are the boys?" asked Chatworth on the telephone.

It was just after lunch, nearly two weeks after the school poisoning.

"Oh, they're fine," said Janet.

"Quite recovered?"

"Yes, of course."

Janet glanced at Roger, who was sitting on the piano stool and reading the morning newspaper. He no longer needed glasses, and his period of caution was over, his eyes were as good as they had ever been. It was the middle of July, a sultry but cloudy day, with occasional drizzle; July had come in wet and was continuing wet; as the jeremiahs had prophesied they were paying for the brilliant spring.

"That's good," said Chatworth gruffly. "Don't worry about them, Janet, I'll see they have a guard with them all the time. Just don't worry. Roger there?"

"Yes, would you like to speak to him?" Janet asked, sweetly and calmly.

"Why d'you think I called?" growled Chatworth.

Roger came across, kissed Janet lightly on the cheek, took the receiver, and dropped down into his chair. He felt perfectly fit, but had not yet been back to the office. Sloan and Peel had kept him up to date with the case, although there was not a great deal to keep up to date with; there had been no developments of any kind since the poisoning at school.

A stranger had been in the school kitchen that morning, on a pretext of looking at the gas stoves; he'd been left alone for ten minutes. No one had been able to describe him properly.

"West speaking, sir," said Roger mildly.

"About time! How are you?"

202

"Fit for work."

"Sure about that?" asked Chatworth.

"The doctors say so, I say so, and the only one who disagrees is my wife," said Roger, as Janet leaned against the piano and made a face at him. "I was planning to come along for an hour or two this afternoon and start in the morning. If that's all right with you."

"It isn't," said Chatworth.

Roger didn't speak. Janet, seeing the change in his expression, stood upright, and looked anxious.

"Why not, sir?"

Roger's voice had a formal edge.

Chatworth chuckled, and relieved the sudden tension. Janet relaxed, Roger leaned back in the chair.

"Because—just a minute," said Chatworth.

Roger covered the mouthpiece with his right hand, and whispered: "I wonder what the old fox is up to now."

He took his hand away, and waited for several seconds, then heard the tail end of Chatworth's voice, addressed to someone in the office.

"...and hurry! Hallo, hallo, Roger!"

"I'm still here."

"Yes. Where was I? Oh, yes—I don't think you ought to come back on official duty until you're sure nothing more will be heard of this case. That means until it's finished. Apart from your troubles, and I don't minimize them, three murders have been committed. We seem to be no nearer catching the murderer than we were the day after they were committed. We've a pile of reports as high as my neck, and they don't help much."

"I've read them all," Roger said flatly. He felt uneasy again; couldn't guess what Chatworth was getting at. "I'd like to get to work on the job myself again, and—"

"That's just the point. Once you come back here you'll have a load of other stuff to cope with. What's more, you'll be telling these people that you're fit again. Why not stay where you are, and work from there? You can do a lot by telephone. If the killers think you're still unfit for duty, they may continue to lay off, and that should give you more time. See what I mean?"

Roger grinned with sudden elation.

"I do!"

"Agree, I hope?"

"It might work," said Roger quietly. "It would be a nice change to start fooling them. So you want me to have a relapse?"

"Something like that. Still attending the eye hospital?"

"I paid my last visit the day before yesterday—officially."

"Pay another," said Chatworth. "Let everyone know that you're worried about your eyes again. If the guess about their intention to blind you is right, and it looks like it, that should satisfy them."

"I'll fix it," Roger promised.

"Good!" Chatworth was brisk, and went on quickly, as if he had completely finished with that subject and was now dealing with something far less important. "Now, Roger, another little thing. Your friend Lessing. I know that he's been doing a lot, I know he's had one or two spots of trouble himself. On the other hand, I'm not happy about his association with Mrs. Wedlake. Are you?"

Roger didn't answer.

"That silence means you're not," said Chatworth blandly. "How did it start? Was he supposed to get friendly with her, to find out what she knew?"

"Yes."

"Well, it's gone a long way past that now. He sees her practically every day. I've had talk with both Sloan and Peel. They're as loyal to Lessing as you are, but they're worried about this business. They're not sure of the woman, certainly not sure that her story's the whole truth. Part of it is; she was married to Clifford Wedlake when she said she was, she worked for Wiseman, too. But her devotion to the Kennedy family isn't reassuring. What's more, she's seeing a lot of Peter Kennedy outside the office—Lessing one night, Kennedy the next. In short, she seems to be playing fast and loose."

"I see," said Roger heavily.

"In the circumstances, I've instructed both Sloan and Peel to withhold all information from Lessing. So must you. You know, don't you, that he probably told Eve Wedlake about the last attack on you, and that's how it got into the Press when it did?"

"It's possible, sir." Roger was very formal. "I doubt if it happened."

"I'd expect you to doubt it. I don't see how else it could have leaked out, all the same."

"The man who sent the letter would have had a shrewd idea," Roger said dryly. "Still it's just possible Mark let something slip."

"From the way he's going on, that woman could make him tell her anything," said Chatworth. "Sorry if he's let himself in for a big jolt, later on. Like him, myself, and I know how you feel about it. All the same, the more I study the reports the more it seems to me that this Wedlake woman is

205

very much an unknown quantity. She used to work for Wiseman; she may, even now. He's still sitting pretty in the South of France, and could be doing this through Mrs. Wedlake and others. Couldn't he?"

"Yes."

"You saw that woman on the promenade at Bournemouth," Chatworth said abruptly. "Could it have been Mrs. Wedlake?"

Roger hesitated.

"Well, could it, or couldn't it?"

Roger said, "Her hair was a different color, and she wore pancake make-up and those big glasses. I couldn't be sure. Obviously it's possible, and I said so in one of my earlier reports."

"Oh, she hasn't pulled any wool over your eyes," said Chatworth bluffly. "But she might have been at Bournemouth; she could have killed Gorley; she could have spoken to the blind men; we don't know exactly where she was at the time they were approached about their job."

Roger said slowly, "Yes, and that's one thing we've overlooked."

"What is?" Chatworth barked.

"The blind men's ability to identify the people who bribed them," answered Roger very softly. "Usually they've remarkable hearing, and can identify sounds much more easily than we can. They have to recognize people by their voices. I don't know how long the sound of a fresh voice stays in their consciousness, but it's worth finding out. We'll let those blind men listen to Mrs. Wedlake's voice. They might be able to say if she was the woman who bribed them."

"Hm, yes," Chatworth conceded. "Go ahead, and

fix it. But, Roger—Mark Lessing isn't himself. Don't rely on him. You know exactly what I mean, don't you?"

"Yes," said Roger.

"That's all for now. Good-by. Keep in touch by telephone. See Sloan and Peel after dark. Don't forget to go back to the eye hospital. I'll have a report circulated for the Press that your eyes are worrying you again. And good luck!"

Chatworth rang off.

It was a relief to sit back and talk to Janet.

This was a brute of a case. At the beginning Mark had appeared to be as much in danger as he; he hadn't been lately. Chatworth hadn't mentioned it, but Roger had noticed what might be a significant fact some time ago. From the time that Mark had begun to see Eve Wedlake frequently, all hint of danger to him had faded. She might have had the power to withdraw the attacks on him. If she were working for Wiseman—or for Kennedy, who could not be ruled out—it would pay her to keep Mark friendly and unhurt.

Janet listened to the story, without moving from the piano stool. There were no other sounds in the house, occasionally a car passed along the street or people walked by. The windows were wide open; sounds traveled clearly.

"Well, what do you make of it?" Roger asked at last.

"Mark is seeing her often," said Janet, "and—we've known him for a long time. He's had *affaires*, but I don't ever remember him being affected as much as he is now. Do you?"

"Pretty nearly." Roger stirred in his chair. "Yes, I do, he—"

"Well, he's never been affected more."

That was true, and Roger couldn't argue about it.

Janet said, "I've been wondering how it would turn out. I'd hate him to have a bad blow, but if this woman proves to be bad, he will have. He's desperately in love, I can see that clearly. I think he knows what might happen and the possibility frightens him. Chatworth's right, darling. What will you do? Just leave things as they are and say nothing, or tell Mark?"

"If I tell him he'll know why we're changing our minds."

"If you say nothing, he'll guess, sooner or later." Janet glanced up, as a car came along the road. It slowed down and she stood up, to look over the garden fence. "I thought so," she said. "It's Mark's car. He would have to come now. Darling, I—"

She broke off, abruptly.

Roger stood up.

"What is it?"

Janet didn't need to say, for Roger saw Eve Wedlake getting out of the car.

21

Deception

As she stood up, her back to the house, she laughed; it was a laugh of sheer delight and good to hear. Mark's voice followed.

Janet turned to Roger.

"What—"

"You let them in," Roger said. "Don't say anything at first, but after they've chatted for ten minutes, I'll make an excuse to get out of the room. When I've gone, tell them you're worried about my eyes. Make them believe it."

Janet said slowly, "I suppose it's the only thing to do. I hate deceiving Mark, but—"

"Let's face facts."

"All right," Janet said decisively, and went to the hall.

Roger sat back in his chair, and didn't look round. He heard the couple coming up the narrow path, no longer laughing but talking freely—the gay, inconsequential talk of lovers. He thought he detected a note of excitement, an underlying emotion more than just gaiety.

Janet opened the door before they rang. Snicker didn't growl, but watched warily. He was in the passage alongside the stairs. Roger thought of him —and another darkling thought flashed into his mind. Mark might be able to influence the dog, might put Eve on good terms with him.

No one spoke to Snicker.

Mark was saying, "I've been wanting you two to meet for a long time. Janet, this is Eve. Eve, you now know the other and better half of the West family!"

He couldn't keep the gaiety out of his voice, nor repress his high spirits.

"Hallo," said Janet; and her smile came easily, she could fool Mark; she could fool anyone. "I hope you realize you can't believe half of what Mark says."

"Most of what he says," said Eve.

"That's right, start slandering me. Where's Roger?"

"He's been having a nap, I think he's awake now."

"Please don't wake him," Eve said quickly.

"He ought to be awake, even if he isn't," said Janet.

She opened the door and peered into the room, as if she weren't certain how she would find Roger. He stood up and yawned, loudly enough for them to hear.

"Visitors," she announced.

"Eh? Oh! Who?"

"Mark and Mrs. Wedlake."

"Good Lord!" said Roger, as if astounded. He stepped forward as the door opened wider, and the couple came in. Eve wore a dark red suit with a white blouse; it fitted her perfectly. All her clothes did. "Why, hallo!"

"Lazy beggar," Mark said. "The modern Nero, sleeping while time burns. How like professionals, isn't it, Eve? Sit back and yawn, while the much maligned amateurs do their work for them."

"What's all this?" Roger asked.

"Simple facts," said Mark. He was certainly bubbling with an excitement which wasn't only to do with Eve. She sat down and crossed her legs, as naturally as if she were an old friend. "Care to listen?"

"I'm waiting," said Roger.

"We've made a move and a big one," Mark said. "Eve and I went into a huddle, some time ago. In short, she was to continue spying on the Kennedys *and* stringing along with me. Peter was the obvious one to work on, and so she's been working on him. Since the row—you heard about their row?"

Mark was almost boyish.

"Oh, yes."

"Well, since then, Peter's been more subdued. For a week or two he was almost humble. Now, he's—"

"Don't joke about it," Eve said quietly. "I think Peter's serious, I don't like fooling him, but—I *must* know the truth. Mr. West, Mark's told me about this mysterious woman who was at Bournemouth and who talked to the blind men. I'm not guilty." Laughter sprang into her eyes. "I don't suppose anyone at Scotland Yard will believe that until it's proved, but I'm not. I think I've found out who is."

"Oh," said Roger, blankly.

Janet, whom the others couldn't see, raised her

eyebrows. Roger felt an absurd desire: that Chatworth could be just outside the door, listening to all this. Would he change his tune?

"You might look excited," Mark said plaintively. "Go on, Eve, tell him the whole story."

"It began with the dog," said Eve. "The mastiff."

Roger didn't speak, but eyed her intently.

"It's a great brute. I'm not usually nervous of dogs, but he scared me," Eve went on. "He's at a little country cottage, near Horsham, Sussex—and acts as a guard for the girl, who lives alone. Some of the time." She leaned forward, and her expression was sober, almost somber. "I feel excited about it, but there's something beastly in helping to track down a murderer. I'm not—used to it."

"You could be wrong this time," Roger said mildly.

Mark looked surprised; Eve didn't show any reaction to that lack of enthusiasm, but went on quietly:

"Of course. I rather hope I am, in some ways. The girl is Mrs. Mavis Hill, a widow. She's a friend of Charles Kennedy. I didn't think Peter knew much about her, until the other day. Peter and I went down to Worthing, on some business for his father, and saw Charles and the girl driving along the road. The dog was in the back of the car. Charles looked as if he wanted to drive straight past us, but couldn't very well. Later Peter told me that Charles has known her for a long time. He keeps her in a country cottage. *She* keeps the mastiff!"

That note of flippancy was forced. Eve seemed to be wholly frank, but obviously had something else on her mind.

"Could you be sure of recognizing the Bournemouth dog if you saw it?" she asked abruptly.

Roger hesitated.

"Surely you could," Mark urged.

"Er—yes. Yes, I think so," Roger brushed his
hand over his forehead and went on. "I don't think
there's much doubt. Have you seen this woman's
dog?"

"Much to Mark's disgust, I went down to the cottage myself this morning. Peter had the address,
but I wanted to make sure that Charles hadn't
given him the wrong one. Mavis Hill is known in
the nearby village, so is the mastiff, although it
seldom leaves the cottage. It does occasionally,
when another boy friend comes to visit her. *He*
drives a Lagonda," Eve added.

Roger had a swift mental picture of a Lagonda
sweeping up the hill from the beach at Bournemouth.

"This seems to show that Charles Kennedy is in
it," Mark said, looking at Roger thoughtfully. "He's
the dark horse of the family, too. I think Eve's gone
as far as she can. Over to you and the Yard, old
chap." He frowned. "Aren't you feeling too good?"

"Eh? Of course, I'm fine. There are one or two
memos upstairs, I'd like to have a look at them—
reports on mastiffs," he added. "What's this address?"

"May Cottage, Hilton, near Horsham—a few
miles off the main London Road, and almost iso-
lated," Eve said.

"Good, thanks."

Roger went out and closed the door.

He went straight upstairs, knowing that Janet
would do exactly what he wanted.

213

This story might be true; it could be the vital clue, or it could simply be a red herring, to get him off Eve's trail. Mark obviously believed it implicitly.

Downstairs, Mark waited until he heard Roger's footsteps in the room above their heads, stood up and looked across at Janet.

"What's the matter, Jan? Isn't he so well?"

"I don't know whether it's his imagination or not, but he thinks his eyes are bothering him again," Janet said. No one would have disbelieved her, she showed just the right amount of anxiety. "He says they ache more than they did—that's why he had a nap to rest them. He gets headaches, too. He hasn't exactly complained of his sight, but—" She broke off. "I've persuaded him to go to the hospital again. He hates the thought of it, he wanted to get to the office tomorrow, but he can't if he feels like this."

Mark said slowly, "That's the devil."

Eve said, "Mrs. West, I can imagine just how you feel. The real justification I have for going on with this now is that I might help to stop more attacks. Your husband probably won't believe it, but I want to do everything I can to help."

"You're doing a lot," Janet assured her.

"I ought to be kicked," growled Mark. "Before I worried him with this, I ought to have made sure that he was all right. I thought--"

"Everyone thought so, until a day or two ago."

"I could still have checked," said Mark. "He'll want to have a go at this himself, and won't be able to. I should have told Peel or Sloan. I suppose I'd better leave it to Roger now."

"I should," Janet advised. She heard Roger com-

214

ing downstairs and added hastily, "Don't tell him I've told you anything about it. That'll only make him worry more."

"All right" Mark nodded.

Eve said, "If there's anything at all we can do to help, you will tell us, won't you?"

Janet looked into her eyes and believed that she saw sincerity in them; and certainly she saw everything that Mark found in her.

Roger came in, and spoke with forced heartiness.

"There certainly wasn't a mastiff owned by a Mrs. Hill on the list of those reported to the Yard," he said. "I'll get in touch with Sloan. Will you be seeing Charles Kennedy tonight?"

"We can't very well," said Eve. "He's gone out— probably to the cottage to see his Mavis."

Eve said they ought to leave, and Roger waited until they had gone before calling the Yard. He was dialing as Janet was calling good-by, outside. Sloan came on the line as the car moved off. Sloan was gruff; he probably knew what Chatworth had done, and guessed that Roger wouldn't think much of it.

He listened.

"I'll get that dog checked," he promised.

"Better leave the brute to me," said Roger. "I'll recognize him again, don't worry about that. Check on the woman Hill. Find out where she was during the business at Bournemouth, and when the blind men were tackled. Find out who the Lagonda-owning boy friend is. Keep the cottage watched; if Charles Kennedy goes there, report it." All the things that needed doing streamed through his mind. "If the girl shows any sign of leaving the cottage, follow her. If there's a risk of losing her, don't let her go—pull her in for questioning. We want those blind men lined up, too, so that they can hear her speak as well as Eve Wedlake. All clear, Bill?"

Sloan laughed.

"You're better!"

"I'm in the middle of a relapse." Roger grinned. "Let me know at once if it's established that Charles Kennedy goes to the cottage regularly."

"Right."

"Thanks. Oh—and tell Chatworth all about how ill I am."

Sloan laughed.

"I know, and he'll know. You want to prove that he's talking out of the back of his neck were Eve Wedlake and Mark are concerned. I hope he is. Be seeing you."

Sloan rang off.

Roger leaned back and laughed; he knew that he might be taking too much for granted, and laughed again. Janet was in the kitchen. He heard the boys in the distance; they had been out to a friend's house, and were due home now. He stood up, called Snicker, and went outside. Snicker walked sedately by his side, the boys saw them, waved and began to run. The policeman then on duty in Bell Street—one was always there—was on the other side of the road, and smiling paternally at the boys' excitement. Snicker began to get frisky, but wouldn't run on unless he were told he could. Roger waited. A car turned into the street from the King's Road end, and came along at a steady pace. The boys were on the other side of the road, and Roger watched them, to see whether they would take any chances; they didn't, but paused at the curb, impatiently.

The car passed.

A man leaned out, with a gun in his hand, and fired three shots. At the first, Snicker yelped; at the second, he groaned. The third bullet struck the pavement, near him. The car engine roared as Roger broke into a run—a hopeless, enraged gesture. The gunman didn't shoot again, but dropped back into the car. And something white flew out from the window. The policeman's whistle was at Roger's lips, the shrill blast startled the boys as much as the shots had.

Richard saw Snicker first.

"Snicker's hurt!" he cried. "Snicker's hurt!"

He came running across.

There was nothing Roger could do to save them from seeing what had happened. A bullet had gone through Snicker's head, another through his body, and blood was trickling from each wound. He lay on his side, mouth slightly open.

Roger picked up the white thing; a typewritten letter addressed to him, in the familiar cream-laid envelope. The type was big, it hadn't been done on Eve Wedlake's machine.

He opened it, and read:

There isn't a thing you can do, West, we can get you whenever we want. Don't forget it.

"And that's true," Roger said savagely. "They came along the street without caring a damn. If they'd shot at me instead of Snicker they could have got me. They could have picked off either of

217

the boys or Janet. That's the size of it. They've the nerve of the Devil and more cunning, and they hate. How they hate! Nearly as much as I hate them." His voice rasped, his face was pale, and his eyes were glittering. He sat in Chatworth's office at the Yard, a little after four o'clock. "I'm going to get them. I'll lead the party down to this cottage tonight, and see the dog and the woman myself."

"Now, Roger—"

"I'm back at the Yard and I'm staying until it's over or I'm thrown out," Roger growled. A dozen Chatworths, the Home Secretary, the whole of the Cabinet could have been there, and he couldn't have stopped himself from talking this way. "This job's been dragging on for nearly four months. Four months! If it goes on much longer, they'll break me, they'll break my wife, and God knows what might happen to the children."

Chatworth sat back and looked at him through his lashes. Then he spoke in a surprisingly mild voice.

"I see, Roger. So you're going to visit this cottage and the woman and her dog."

"Yes."

"Although you know that if the Wedlake woman is mixed up in this, she probably gave Lessing that information so as to make sure you'd go down there."

"Yes."

"And what then?"

"If it's the same dog and the same woman, I'm going to search Kennedy's flat, his office, and the Guildford country cottage. Charles Kennedy uses each place, that will give us plenty of excuse. We can't search them until we have clear evidence that Charles knows the Hill woman and visits her frequently."

"No, that's true enough." Chatworth picked up a cheroot, but didn't light it. "Roger, listen to me. You're angry, and I don't blame you. The trouble is, in a mood like this you could do something that would spoil the chances of winning, and might injure you and your family. You're not able to judge dispassionately, and that's dangerous."

Roger said, "I'm going to stop creeping round corners and pulling my punches because something might happen to Janet or the boys. Something has, and it can go on happening. It won't stop until we've found the swine behind it. We've stalled around too much. We've tried to be clever. We've watched and waited—and the other side's acted just whenever it wanted to. They started out to get me on the defensive, and they did it so easily they must be sitting back and laughing their heads off. They've put the whole Yard on the defensive, including you. It's time to stop it."

Chatworth looked at him straight, then lit his cheroot with great deliberation, and said: "Maybe you're right. Go ahead. Oh—take guns, you may need them."

It was nearly ten o'clock when Roger's car pulled up in a by-road near the cottage at Horsham. He had spent a lot of time at the Yard, and as far as they could find, Eve's story was true.

Sloan was behind him, a Horsham Inspector at

his side. As they got out of the car, a man came forward out of the trees near by.

"All quiet, sir," he said.

It was a Horsham man.

"Let's go," said Roger.

22

The Cottage

A light shone from a ground-floor window at the cottage. Nothing moved, except the leaves of the trees and the shrubs and long grass near by, as the wind stirred them. The cottage itself was silent. It was surrounded by a low fence, with a small gate opening onto a narrow path which led to the front door. In the darkness the charm of the place was hidden; yet the glow of light gave a hint of it. No other building was within a mile. The only approach was a rutted track which ran past the gate and turned sharply to the left. There was no telephone and no electricity.

Roger and the Horsham man reached the gate together. Yard men and Horsham police had closed in, and now surrounded the garden. There was another gate leading to the back of the cottage and, at one side, a big shedlike garage.

"All set?" Roger asked.

"On a whistle the men will close in."

"Good. We'll have a look at the garage first, I think."

Roger opened the gate, and it creaked noisily. He stepped through, and left it open. No one stirred inside the cottage, and there was no sound. Snicker would have been growling by now; perhaps the mastiff was growling inside. Roger took three steps along the gravel path, then went on to the grass. He walked silently across it, the Horsham man by his side. They had to cross more gravel to reach the garage. The double doors were closed but not locked. The men opened them, and they creaked far worse than the gate—but still nothing stirred at the cottage.

The shape of a small car showed.

Roger switched on his torch. The powerful beam shone on the black bodywork of the car. He bent down, looked at the rear number plate, and gave a soft laugh as he straightened up.

"There are three—interchangeable. One of the neatest arrangements I've come across for using false number plates and changing them on the road. They probably work by a switch. We've found something all right."

"Think this is the Austin you're after?"

"Well, it's an Austin."

Roger went farther forward, shone the torch on the front of the car and saw the unmistakable bonnet lines. He glanced inside. The car was empty except for the usual oddments. He felt the radiator, and it was cool, not cold.

"It must have come in just before we had your call to watch the place," said the Horsham man.

"Yes. Well, we'll try the cottage. Mind if I go first?"

"We ought to go together."

Roger smiled in the gloom.

"Yes, I know. Stick your neck out if you want to, but I'd rather you were lying back, as first reserve."

"Well—all right."

"Thanks."

Roger went across the grass again, toward the front door. The silence and lack of movement seemed uncanny. He reached the gravel of the path in front of the door, and stepped onto it; he couldn't avoid making some noise. There was no sound of the dog. He crept toward the lighted window, and, keeping close to the wall, peered through. At first he saw only the oak beams stretching across the ceiling and the walls; the red-brick fireplace; the powerful paraffin lamp, standing on a small gate-leg table. The cottage had charm, and this was a large room, with window seats, polished oak floor, and Persian rugs. It looked quiet and serene.

He went nearer, and saw the mastiff, stretched out by the fireplace. At first, he saw nothing unusual about it; and then he saw the smear of red on a newspaper near the huge dog's head. It was blood; peering more intently, he could see the wound at the side of the dog's throat.

No one seemed to be in the room. His heart thumped as he crossed to the other side of the window. Two winged armchairs had their backs to the window; someone might be sitting in one of them.

Who would sit calmly with a dead dog in front of them?

From the other side he saw the woman's legs, bent at the knees, and one arm, the elbow rested against an arm of the chair. He could just see the fair hair which fell over her cheek; her attitude, as

223

far as he could judge from here, was easy and natural.

Would a sleeping woman sit so close to a dead
mastiff?

He moved away and beckoned the Horsham
man, who came quietly across the grass. Roger
joined him on the edge of it, told him what he had
seen, in a whisper which seemed just a sighing
sound on the quiet night.

"Think the woman's dead, too?"

"Could be. There's no light in any other part of
the house. I don't get it. She could have killed the
dog and then herself, but why?" Roger didn't try to
answer the question, but went on, "We'll break in
the back way, I think, and—"

He broke off.

His back was to the window, and he looked over
the dark countryside. Here and there, in the distance, he saw a speck of light from a lonely house
or cottage. He could see traffic moving along the
main road, picking out each car from the tiny glow
of the headlights; and he saw a car coming toward
the cottage. It might be traveling along this narrow road to some other place; it was certainly
coming this way.

The Horsham detective turned and watched.

The headlights drew nearer, and soon they could
see where it silvered the branches of trees, and
turned leaves to a pale, translucent green. It was
traveling at speed, and bumping up and down;
they could see it swaying. Soon the smooth beat of
the powerful engine came within earshot.

"It's coming here, all right," the Horsham man
said.

"Let's take cover. Your men won't show themselves, will they?"

"They'll have me to deal with if they do."

They drew back, under the cover of trees which grew close to the corner of the cottage. The headlights swept the nearby trees, but not the waiting men; all were concealed. As it rounded a bend, it showed up the gate of the cottage, took the color out of the flowers in the beds surrounding the lawn, and then turned onto the front door. It showed the ramblers growing over it, the thatched porch, more of its charm. Then the beams lost the cottage, the car drew up near the gate, and the engine stopped.

A man got out, slammed the door, and walked toward the cottage. As he reached the path he stood in the glow of his own sidelights. He was tall and powerful, and moved easily; it was Charles Kennedy.

Halfway along the path Charles broke the quiet with a cheerful, "Hallo, there!" There was no answer. He called again, reached the front door, and beat a sharp tattoo on it with his clenched fist; nothing stirred. His back was toward the watching men, they couldn't see his face properly. He put his right hand to his pocket, and a moment later inserted a key in the lock. As he opened it he called clearly:

"Mavis. Where are you?"

He stepped inside, and the only light was from the inside, which showed the room he'd entered; there was no hall.

"Mavis!"

"Come on," whispered Roger.

They left their hiding place and went forward across the grass, making little sound. As they drew within sight of the window, they saw Charles Kennedy approach the winged chair in which the girl was sitting. It was difficult to judge his expression; all they could see clearly was his set lips and narrowed eyes.

He bent down.

"*Mavis.*"

They could just hear the hoarse voice. His hand moved, as if to touch the woman, and then he drew back. He stared at the window—at Roger and the Horsham man, had he been able to see them?

Then another man spoke, from behind him.

"Don't move, Kennedy."

Roger saw Charles Kennedy turn his head, then stepped nearer the front door; he couldn't see the man from there. Roger was within a few feet of the door, but the gravel lay between him and the door itself, and with men as near as Kennedy and the other, any sound he made would be heard. He stepped onto the gravel, as the man who had spoken said: "Okay, now. Move back to the fireplace. Don't try any tricks, this gun works."

Charles moved toward the fireplace; Roger caught a glimpse of him then. Roger's right hand was tight about the butt of his gun. He stayed where he was, by the side of the door. He couldn't see the man speaking to Kennedy.

Charles said in a rough voice, "Did you kill her?"

Roger took another step forward, on the gravel, under cover of the words.

"Supposing I did—what are you going to do about it?" the other sneered.

Roger took two steps forward; the voice might drown the slight sound he made, and the two men were concentrating on each other, they wouldn't suspect that the police were near.

"I'll show you what I'm going to do," said Charles savagely.

Roger was halfway across the path when he finished.

The man who held a gun unseen laughed; an ugly sound. Silence followed, and then Charles Kennedy began to curse. The torrent came out viciously in a grating voice, as if all the pent-up fury were coming out. Under cover of it Roger reached the door. He took his gun from his pocket and peered through. This was the big room—and a tall man was inside, dark-clad and dark-haired, standing almost sideways to Roger, but a little way in front of him—he couldn't see the open door without turning his head.

Charles stopped.

"Words," sneered the tall man. "What good will they do you? I know you now, Kennedy. I know your game. I've been doing your work for you, and what have you been paying me? Not much, have you? You've put the black on me and made me do it—sure, I know. You've worked through this dame, you didn't think I'd find out you were behind it. Well, I have, see. See her face? It hurt her, when I made those bruises. I came down here to take further orders from her, but I wasn't having any. It was I who telephoned you from Horsham afterward, and told you she wanted to see you. Then I came back and put the car in the garage so that you wouldn't know I was here. Clever, wasn't it?"

Charles didn't speak.

"Lost your tongue?" sneered the man. His voice rose. "Don't move!"

Roger couldn't see Charles; the Horsham man might be at the window again, but there was no sound. After a pause the tall man relaxed, and gave the harsh laugh again.

"That's better. You forgot something, Kennedy. You forgot I've got a *mind*. I can think, get it? I can think for myself. I'll tell you some of the things I've been thinking. I passed on your orders to Doc Gorley, didn't I? He passed them on to Marino, and Marino passed them on to Bertie Downs. That was smart—none of them could give more than one of the others away. Then Downs died. Then Marino. Then I had to kill Gorley—and you tried to double-cross me about Gorley's death."

Charles said harshly, "You're crazy."

"I'm not so crazy."

"You're crazy and you're wrong. The police were after Gorley; if he'd talked, you would have been finished. I gave you a chance to get rid of him and to frame the Wedlake woman."

"I did all I could!"

"Oh, sure. And then you reminded me that I killed Gorley, so I'd better do what you say. Your Mavis told me that much. She told me there wasn't a thing I could do to protect myself. If I didn't go on taking orders, I'd find myself in dock. She threatened to squeal—the same way as she's been putting on the squeeze for months. Well, I've been squeezed dry. So I made her tell me who worked with her. You went too far, Kennedy, when you tried that last squeeze. What are you getting out of all this?"

Charles said, "Never mind that."

"But I do mind," said the other softly. "I—"

"*You're* getting plenty," Charles Kennedy said in his new, harsh voice. "West put you inside for seven years, didn't he? Thanks to me you're getting a chance to give him hell in return, and—"

"That's not so much. I want plenty more, Kennedy—and I want to know why you're doing it—why Mavis told me to put the squeeze on your father. I want to know everything. Understand? I want to know because there's big money in it, and I want a share of that money. You wouldn't do this if there wasn't big money in it. Give."

"There's nothing. I—"

The roar of a shot rang out, loud and clear. Roger saw the flash, started, and moved forward. He heard a rustle of movement behind him, but the Horsham man didn't come far. The echoes of the shot died, and the little man said: "Now you know I'm serious. What's in it, Kennedy? Do you reckon you'll get that hundred thousand smackers out of your old man? Because if you can, *I* can."

Charles didn't speak.

The man laughed on a sneering note.

"You needn't stall, and you needn't hope you'll be rescued. You've got just one chance of living. Tell me what you've got on your old man. Tell me how *I* can squeeze the dough out of him. Then maybe I'll give you a chance. Not such a big chance. I'll leave you here with the corpse, until I've seen your old man and got what I want. *If* he pays up, I'll tell him where to find you. If he doesn't—"

He broke off.

"Benson, listen." Charles sounded desperate. "I tell you—"

"Stay where you are!"

"Listen to me. My father hasn't got a hundred thousand, you won't gain anything if I talk to you. I can find a thousand pounds for you. I'll pay you in the morning, after the banks are open. I can't do any more. I—"

"You'll talk," sneered Benson. *"Keep still!"*

There was a scuffle of movement.

Roger fired, from the hip, as another flame spurted from Benson's gun and he heard Charles rushing forward. Benson staggered and his gun dropped, he gaped toward the door. Roger stepped over the threshold. As he entered the room there was a thud; he was in time to see Charles Kennedy fall forward on his face. Roger pushed past Benson as the Horsham man came through the door. Outside, a whistle shrilled, and the police started to close in.

Benson fell against a chair, and lost his balance.

Charles Kennedy lay on the floor, face downward, quite still. The girl sat in the chair with her throat cut; as the dog's was cut.

The Horsham man reached Benson, whose right arm hung limp by his side. Outside, the police were shouting. One called clearly to another: "Kennedy's dead! So—so is the woman!"

Then a car started up, startling everyone. Men out there shouted again, and one came rushing in.

"What's on?" demanded Roger.

"There was another man in that car, hiding in the back. He's driving off." The policeman was breathless.

"Stop him," growled the Horsham man. "Don't stand there!"

But the unknown man who had come with Charles Kennedy was already a long way off.

Benson's bullet had caught Charles Kennedy between the eyes; he must have been dead before he hit the ground.

Roger sat in the office of the Horsham Superintendent, papers spread out in front of him, sandwiches and tea on a tray near the telephone, the receiver in his hand. He was waiting for Sloan to come through. The Horsham Inspector who had been with him, a pale, flabby man, was sitting at the other side of the desk.

Roger said, "Hallo, Bill?"

"You okay, Roger?"

"I'm fine. We're getting places, and, for the record, it's because of the information Eve Wedlake lodged." He grinned, but that didn't linger. "Listen, Bill. We've got the man with the bowler had and the Austin. It's Kib Benson, remember him? We put him inside for seven years, for robbery with violence. We didn't know he'd killed a couple of men then. Charles Kennedy did, and blackmailed Benson into doing most of the attacking jobs—including all the shooting in the street. Benson was at Bournemouth with the Hill woman. He found the blind man to whom she spoke. He killed Gorley—he'd been giving Gorley orders. Gorley got that arsenic, and Benson still has a supply in his car—the Austin."

He paused.

Sloan said in a tense voice, "I've got all that. Anything else?"

"Not yet. According to Benson, Charles Kennedy was behind the pressure on his father. Benson did the jobs, but took his orders from this Hill woman. She was working for Charles, Benson was driven too far, and he made her talk tonight. She told him that she got her orders from Charles, and Charles practically admitted it. We'd be right home, I think, if Benson hadn't killed both the woman and Charles."

"*What?*"

"Yes, it's that bad."

"Was Charles working with anyone else?"

"That's what we have to find out. He had another man with him tonight, but we lost him. They were driving a Lagonda, presumably the car kept at Mavis Hill's cottage. There's a call out, of course. Is Peel still watching the Deverall Court flat?"

"Yes," said Sloan, and paused, probably to try to digest something of what he'd heard. "Yes—he rang up ten minutes ago. Mark and the Wedlake woman went in about ten o'clock. It's turned eleven-fifteen now. Peter's not there, we aren't sure where he is. Clara's at home, of course." The "of course" was casual; Clara never left Jacob Kennedy alone if she could help it. "Going to raid the flat?"

"Later. I'm going across to Jacob Kennedy's Guildford cottage, it's a short cut across country from here, we'll do it in half an hour. I'll have a look round there. If anyone leaves the flat send 'em back."

"Including Mark?"

"Yes."

"All right," said Sloan slowly. "It's beginning to look as if Eve Wedlake's on the up-and-up, if she hadn't told us this—"

"Supposing we wait until we know everything?" Roger said. "I'll be back as soon as I can. Oh, telephone Janet, will you? Tell her everything's fine, and it's nearly over. Oh, another thing—we've found the other typewriter, the one with the bigger type, at the cottage here. We've also found that Jacob Kennedy owns the cottage."

"Meaning what?"

"We'll find out," said Roger. The Horsham man was signaling to him and mouthing words, and he broke off, "Hold on a minute, will you?"

He put his hand over the mouthpiece.

"You've forgotten—the Hill woman," said the Horsham man.

Roger grinned.

"I like leaving the tastiest bit at the end for Bill Sloan. Hallo, Bill! There's one other thing which means we mustn't believe too much what Eve Wedlake's told us, yet. We looked through the papers at the cottage, and found a birth certificate. Mavis Hill was born Mavis Wedlake."

Sloan cried, *"What's* that?"

"She would be just about the right age to be Eve's sister-in-law, wouldn't she?" asked Roger.

23

Discovery at Guildford

Roger sat beside a Yard detective officer who was driving Roger's car, and closed his eyes. They were traveling at a good speed through the deserted countryside. It was after eleven; things had happened quickly, but Roger wasn't yet sure that they had happened quickly enough. He was pleasantly tired, and his spirits were higher than they had been for a long time. He did not think there would be any more serious trouble; the nightmare possibility of attacks on Janet and the boys had gone, or nearly gone. He wished that man hadn't driven off from the cottage. Had it been Peter Kennedy? Benson had filled in so many gaps, but hadn't filled in them all.

Roger opened his eyes and sat up, lit a cigarette, and asked: "How far to go, Wilson?"

"Should be there in ten minutes, now, sir."

"Good. Any ideas about this job yourself?"

In his Detective Officer days he'd bristled with ideas, and no one had been interested.

Wilson took his eyes off the road for a moment, and grinned.

"I couldn't say I have, sir, except about the Wedlake woman. She's too good to be true. She's a dream, and I don't believe in dreams. I've given a lot of thought to the Kennedy family, and I always thought Charles was the worst of the bunch. I'd only just been promoted to the C.I.D. branch when that case was on, helped you with some of the preliminaries, if you remember, sir."

"Oh, I remember."

"Not much you forget, is there?" asked Wilson. "Do you think Charles was alone in it?"

"I don't know."

"I can't imagine why he should put the black on his own father," mused Wilson. "But it makes one thing pretty certain—that Jacob Kennedy has plenty salted away somewhere. Who'd be more likely to know it than his own son? It looks as if Charles wanted to get his hands on every pound he could, and worked this business out. If there's a crook worse than most, it's one who'll work on his own family."

"Ah, yes," murmured Roger.

Wilson glanced away from the road again. A rabbit darted from one hedge to that opposite, and showed up clearly, tail bobbing up and down, white as snow. The car traveled smoothly. They were on a hill, very near Guildford now, and could see the lights of the town, and of villages not far away. This was a side road, and they had passed little traffic on the way. Two more cars were behind them, with two Yard men in each.

"Think you know why he did it?" asked Wilson.

"I'd just make a guess, and kick myself if I were wrong," said Roger. "We're pretty near the answer though. I know the way to the cottage—pull up and let me take over, will you?"

Wilson pulled up, secretly convinced that West knew a lot more than he had said. The other cars slowed down, and they had a five minutes' breather and a conference, Roger doing most of the talking. Tactics would be the same as at Horsham, and they were to meet the Guildford police near Kennedy's cottage.

The tactics weren't necessary, for the second cottage was empty. No one had been here for several days. Roger and a local man forced entry at the back door, and began a systematic search. The "cottage" was actually a nine-roomed house, but the police were in strength enough to split up the work and to save time. Roger chose the study-cum-library, a small room lined with books and, like the rest of the house, furnished with extremely good taste and regardless of expense. There was a big pedestal desk, of walnut; it was easy to open the drawers, but they found nothing of interest. They found a wall safe behind the desk, and without the combination number it would take some opening. In fact, it was the last thing they attempted, and a Yard expert on safes was working at this while others looked through the books. The rest of the rooms were finished; Charles Kennedy had his own room and a few private papers here, but nothing which helped. The whole party concentrated on the study, taking down each book, and shaking it with the pages open, to make sure nothing was hidden.

Roger saw a man turning over larger books than

most, with thick pages. He moved across, pausing by the man at the safe, who was turning the knob and listening to the tumblers falling. He shook his head—he hadn't found the combination yet.

"What are these?"

Roger picked up one of the big books.

"Books in Braille, sir."

Roger said softly, "Well, well, books in Braille."

"That's right, sir." Wilson looked puzzled, and certainly saw nothing really significant in it. "Nothing inside them at all."

"Well, well," said Roger again. "Take them all out to my car, will you? Anything else here to do with blindness?"

"I haven't seen anything."

Roger raised his voice, and everyone paused.

"If you come across books on blindness, the eyes, vision, or anything like that, put them aside, will you?" There was a murmur of acknowledgment, and he glanced along several shelves which had already been examined. He found nothing. He went to the telephone and dialed the Yard. Sloan had left for Deverall Street, another Inspector took his request.

"Look up the prison reports on Kennedy and Wiseman, will you, and put them on my desk."

"Right, Handsome."

"Thanks."

Roger rang off, and Wilson came back as the man at the safe said: "Got it!"

Roger swung round. The safe was open, and the Yard man rubbed his hands together with self-satisfaction.

"Nice work," said Roger. "Let's have a look."

There was not a great deal in the safe. A cash

box, which wasn't locked; there were fifty pounds in it, and a few oddments in foreign currency; two or three small notebooks and some other papers. Roger took them to the desk, glanced through one of the books. There were a number of entries, and each page had the address of someone abroad; in all, there were eleven foreign names and addresses. The entries were in figures. The French and Italian figures ran into hundreds of thousands, most of the others were much smaller but never less than tens of thousands.

"Anything any good?" asked Wilson.

"Oh, I think so," Roger said softly. "We're having quite a night out. Look at these—nearly seven million is the total in Paris. If that means seven million francs, it means that Kennedy probably has seven thousand pounds salted away in France. Eight million in Italy—let's say six thousand pounds, if they represent lira. A hundred thousand in Switzerland—Swiss francs are worth about two bob each, aren't they?—that makes pretty well ten thousand pounds in Switzerland."

Wilson's eyes were glowing.

"So he's still in the foreign-currency racket."

"It could be. We'll ask him a question or two about these."

Roger put the book aside, and opened a file of papers. He whistled as he read, said nothing, put the papers aside, and looked up at a man going through another set of papers.

"Got anything?"

The man grinned. "Have I! Dossiers on several people, including you, sir. Mr. Lessing, too. Mrs. Wedlake and Mavis Wedlake, Benson, Gorley— quite a lot. He knew pretty well all there was to know about everyone—age, circumstances, history. We couldn't do much better at the Yard."

"Yes, it's quite a night, isn't it?" Roger chuckled as he glanced through the papers. "Now, I think we—"

He broke off, at a shout outside. Then someone ran heavily along the drive toward the road; two or three others followed. The engine of a car started up. Roger hurried to the front door, and was in time to see a man climb into a car and drive off. Torches shone out from the watching policemen, and showed the man's face clearly.

"Get him!" Roger cried. "That's Peter Kennedy."

He reached his car before any of the others.

They lost Peter Kennedy on the other side of Guildford. Roger stopped at an Automobile Association box, used his key, and telephoned the Yard. Sloan was back.

"Wait at the Deverall Court flat for Peter Kennedy, Bill. If he turns up before I get there, keep him out. If I'm there first, we'll have a chat then."

"Right!" said Sloan.

"Mark still with the Kennedys?"

"Yes, he's having a late session."

"It won't last much longer," Roger said. "Bill, phone Chelsea. Tell them to put every available man on Bell Street in case Peter has a final stab. Oh, he's in it. I'll be at Deverall Court in an hour."

In fact, he took an hour and five minutes, and arrived just after one-thirty. Sloan and Peel were outside Deverall Court, and everything was quiet. Lights still shone from the front-room windows.

"Peter back?" asked Roger as he climbed out of his car.

"No—no change. Why the hell Mark's staying there as late as this I can't begin to guess."

"We'll soon find out," said Roger grimly. "Let's get in."

By eleven o'clock that evening Mark Lessing was able to understand exactly why Eve felt so certain that Jacob Kennedy knew nothing of the vendetta. For a man with an ugly reputation, and one suspected of a part in the crimes which had kept the Yard on edge for months, he had a surprisingly likable personality. There was a likable quality about Clara, too, more obvious when one got to know her. In her birdlike way she was attractive. She had a keen sense of humor, and that night seemed to be much happier than she had been for some time. Or was her gaiety forced?

They had played bridge until ten minutes to eleven; Kennedy and Clara, with all the cards, were fifteen and sixpence to the good.

"It's time we had a drink," Jacob Kennedy said. He stood up, moved toward a cocktail cabinet in a sumptuously furnished room, with a green-and-gold *decor*, and Mark glanced at Eve. She looked relaxed and at her best, as gay and vivacious now as she had been earlier in the evening. Then suddenly she frowned, and started up.

Mark turned to look at Kennedy.

He was standing a few feet from the cocktail cabinet, one hand stretched out, the other at his forehead, as if he had suddenly been taken ill. Clara called out sharply, and jumped up. As she ran toward him, Kennedy snatched his hand away from his forehead, and said abruptly:

"I'm all right. Don't fuss. Don't *fuss!*"

240

It was the first time he had spoken roughly all the evening, and he shook Clara's hand off. She stood a little way from him, anxious, staring.

"Pretend to notice nothing," Eve whispered to Mark.

"What is it?"

"He has occasional attacks, I don't know what the trouble is."

"Whisky, Lessing?" asked Kennedy in a stronger voice; it was as if he were proving that he was perfectly all right, by speaking a little too loudly.

"Please."

"What about you, Eve?"

"May I have gin?"

"Jake, why don't you go and sit down?" asked Clara fussily. "I can do that, you look as if you've a headache."

She took a bottle from his hand and put it aside, gripped his arm firmly and made him go to a chair. He dropped into it willingly enough, leaned back, and closed his eyes. He looked very pale.

"And a whisky for you," said Clara perkily. "I know what's good for you!" She gave a little clucking laugh; now that Kennedy was doing what she wanted, she also pretended that nothing was the matter. "I wish the boys would come, it's getting late."

"You fuss too much," said Kennedy, more naturally. "It's not twelve yet—is it?"

He glanced at his wrist watch.

"Nearly a quarter-past eleven," Clara said quickly. Whisky gurgled into glasses, and she took Kennedy's to him first. "I suppose it isn't late, but I can't help worrying about them. Peter hasn't been himself lately, and I wish Charles wouldn't stay away at night so often. He stays out *too* often, and—"

"He's thirty," Kennedy said simply.

"He's still young enough to act like a fool."

"Aren't we all?" Kennedy asked. He put his glass to his lips, slowly, turned his head toward Mark, and smiled. "Better luck with the cards next time, Lessing."

"Thanks."

Clara brought Eve a gin-and-orange.

"I ought to be going," Mark said, as he sipped.

"Oh, don't go yet." Kennedy spoke quite easily. "We never go to bed until after midnight—seldom, anyhow. Clara likes to wait for the boys, if she knows they're coming home. Peter is, tonight—he would have said if he weren't. Charles wasn't sure, was he, Clara?"

"He's *never* sure," said Clara. "I can't think what's come over him lately, he's so secretive. But what am I thinking of! You must all be famished, there are some snacks in the kitchen."

She bustled out, and Kennedy laughed.

"She's on the go from the time she gets up until she goes to bed, and regards sleep as a waste of time."

"I'll go and lend her a hand," Eve said.

"Don't worry, the maid left everything—" Kennedy broke off, for Eve was already at the door. She closed it after her, and Kennedy laughed as he put his glass down. It touched the edge of the table and nearly fell, and he steadied it and pushed it farther on. He looked straight at Mark; and his eyes were heavy, as if he had a severe headache. "Now we've a minute or two alone, Lessing, I'd

242

like to have a word with you. You won't mind if I take an old man's license, will you?"

Mark chuckled.

"Old?"

"That's right, old. It's about you and Eve, of course. I won't pretend that I'm not sorry she's so obviously interested in you. I hoped that she and Peter would make a match of it, I think they would have done had Peter had a little more sense. Still, there it is. Eve hasn't worked for me for very long, but I've become very fond of her."

Mark didn't speak.

"Look after her," said Kennedy. "Give her plenty of rope. She won't be driven, she hates discipline, but she's one of the most efficient women I've ever known, and she manages to be efficient without thrusting her worth down your throat. She—"

The telephone bell rang.

Kennedy started. He was within easy reach of the telephone, and stretched out his hand, missed it the first time, then gripped it tightly.

"Hallo?"

The door opened, and Clara appeared, empty-handed. Anxious?

"Are you—" she began, then stopped and watched.

Kennedy listened, finally said softly, "Oh, that's all right, thanks very much." He put down the receiver and said: "It's nothing—nothing, my dear."

It was a palpable lie.

Clara, watching him closely, knew that. Mark sensed it. Kennedy's eyes closed, he looked as if he had received a blow from which he would never properly recover. He didn't move, but stared at Clara, and the color drained from her face. She turned away abruptly, and hurried across the hall to the kitchen.

Mark lit a cigarette: the quicker he left, the better; that was obvious now. Kennedy wasn't well—and yet Kennedy had had a shock. If he could find out a little more—

Clara came bustling in, her face pasty white and her eyes feverishly bright. She carried a tray with coffee and cups, milk and sugar. She crossed the room, and put the tray down at a table near Kennedy's side.

"Mark—come and lend me a hand," Eve called.

Mark went out, but didn't close the door. He thought that Clara stared intently at her husband; knew that she was sure that he'd received bad news. Mark went across the hall, and met Eve at the kitchen door.

"Mark, what's happened?"

"There was a telephone call, and—"

"Yes, I know. Clara came back, looking as if she would faint. She got herself under control but she's absolutely living on her nerves. Mark, if you could tackle them the right way now, I think they would talk."

"Problem—what's the right way?" Mark turned, frowning, and walked quietly across to the door of the big room.

He heard a single word, from Clara.

"*Dead*," she said.

It was like a groan.

Kennedy didn't speak.

There was a moment's silence, then Clara moved; her bustling movements were unmistakable. Mark went back into the kitchen, and Eve gave him two plates of sandwiches. He was halfway across the hall when Clara came out. Her eyes were little burning balls, and she stared at him, but hardly seemed to notice him. She went into a bedroom, closing the door behind her.

Eve whispered, "What did you hear?"

"Nothing good."

Mark went into the big room. Kennedy was sitting back with his eyes closed; he'd looked pale before, now he looked as if he were on the point of collapse.

Mark put the plates down, went across, and stood near the older man. Eve followed him, quietly.

Mark said, "Mr. Kennedy, if you'll try to forget that I'm a friend of the police, and tell me what the trouble is, I may be able to help. What's gone wrong?"

Kennedy didn't speak.

Clara spoke from the door, in a curiously strained voice.

"What's gone wrong? *I'll* tell you. Charles is dead. Killed. Your kind friend West. Don't move! Don't move, either of you."

She covered Eve and Mark with an automatic.

24

Call for West

Clara stood with her back to the door, and the automatic was steady. It pointed toward Mark, could shift the moment that Eve moved. Clara was too far away for Mark to hope to strike the gun from her hand. Her eyes were still burning, her lips were turned back, she looked vicious—evil.

Kennedy got up slowly.

"Clara, what—" began Eve.

"Keep your mouth shut!"

"But I don't understand."

"You'll understand soon enough, you beauty. You'll understand that it doesn't pay to spy on us. Oh, we know your game. We've always known. You'd found out about Charles and Mavis, hadn't you? You put the police on to the cottage, you sent West there."

Eve said, "I still don't understand. Mavis?"

"You lying little shrew. Mavis! That's right, Mavis Hill, your precious sister-in-law, your husband's beautiful sister. *You* discovered where she was. You knew she worked with Charles, you came to find out all you could. Think we didn't know? We knew from the beginning, but we let you stay, my pretty. You were useful to us, someone for West to suspect. You—"

"All right, my dear," interrupted Kennedy. His face was a mask; all expression had gone, except from his eyes, and they burned, like his wife's. "We'll wait until we hear from Peter, and then—"

"Why wait? If they've killed Charles they'll go to Guildford. We've known it might happen any time, and now it's happened. There's only one thing left."

The woman spat the words out.

"We'll wait a little while," Kennedy said.

He went close to Mark, careful not to stand between him and the gun—and suddenly struck him across the eyes. Mark staggered back, Eve put out a hand to support him, and Kennedy pushed her away. It was controlled violence; he didn't follow it up.

Mark's eyes were streaming.

"Feel that?" asked Kennedy, in a sneering voice. "Your eyes *hurt*, don't they? They have before, and they will again, I'll put them out. Understand, I'll put them out. Yours and West's."

"Don't wait!" Clara cried.

"Not long," said Kennedy.

Eve said thinly, "Jacob, why on earth—"

"Just keep quiet, Eve," said Kennedy. "I didn't think it would come about, but I really like you. Clara never has, but I do. I've always known why you came to work for us. I know that you always wanted to find out what had happened to your husband's money, that you thought you would find something from us. *And* I know that you were looking for his sister. Well, you won't find her, she's dead, too."

"Mavis?" Clara said shrilly. "Dead?"

"Yes, both of them. Peter was with Charles, but the police didn't see him. He let Charles go on first to talk to Mavis, and was going to get out when he saw a policeman near by. He hid in the car, and heard a man call out that Charles—Charles and Mavis were dead. Peter has gone on to Guildford. If the police go there he'll telephone us. West was at Horsham, of course."

Kennedy spoke softly, as if every word was an effort. Mark made himself speak. "Eve, what is this?"

"I'll tell you what it is," said Kennedy. "Her husband lost all his money through making investments on his sister's advice. Mavis advised Cliff Wedlake to deal with us, because Charles worked on her. She was always in love with Charles. Eve discovered that. Eve—"

Eve said quietly, "I liked Mavis, Mark. Her husband was killed soon after mine, and I lost sight of her—I'd promised Cliff to look after her. She was like Cliff in some ways, weak and foolish, but—the Kennedys or someone had turned her bad. I thought that Charles was involved, but didn't know about the others. Until tonight I didn't think that Jacob knew anything about it."

"Well, I knew," Jacob Kennedy told her softly. "I fooled you—all the time, in every way. You aren't so clever, my dear. No one has menaced *me*. Not really. Charles made a man named Benson send threats and menaces and demands by letter and telephone, but that was to fool you, my dear. So that you would pass it on to Lessing or the police.

248

We put you up to getting to know Lessing. We even pinned a message to your flat door, and staged the attack outside your flat, to make West think that I was being threatened by the same people who were threatening him. The scene between me and Peter was to fool West, too. Peter and I always used Eve's typewriter, to make worse confusion and throw suspicion on to you. Wasn't it nicely worked out? West suspected me from the beginning and put Lessing on to watching me, so I made him think I was in the same boat as himself. We made him suspect you. We gave him Gorley to look for. We kept stabbing at him, and put the fear of death into him—I said I would, in the dock, and I *have*. I'll do worse to him, yet. He's been lucky twice, escaped blinding twice, but the third time—I'll do it."

Clara broke in harshly: "And Lessing!"

"Yes, and Lessing," Kennedy said.

Eve asked fiercely, "But why? West only did his job, and Lessing—"

"Because they blinded *me*," said Kennedy in a quivering voice. "I'm going blind. It started in prison. I saw several doctors, they all said nothing could be done, that an operation wouldn't help. Since I came out I've seen the best specialists in the world, including an American ophthalmologist. Know what he said? He said that he could have saved my sight with an operation if I'd gone to him earlier. He also said it was too late now. So—*West* blinded me by sending me—"

He broke off, then went on very slowly. "At times I have such pain in my eyes that it nearly drives me mad. I had spells of it in prison, but they've been more frequent lately. I had an attack, just now.

"Yes, I'm going blind." His voice dropped to a whisper. "And when I realized that it was too late to do anything to save myself, I decided to blind both West and Lessing. And to give them a taste of the hell they'd made for me."

Eve said, "You're not sane."

"Supposing you stop talking," Clara said shrilly. "Jake, I think—"

The telephone bell rang again. Mark saw Kennedy start, saw the older woman glance toward the instrument. He took his chance then; there probably wouldn't be another. He snatched up one of the coffee pots and hurled it across the room at the woman. As he did so, Kennedy turned and hit him, a vicious blow in the face, then kicked him in the groin. As he doubled up and Eve jumped forward, Kennedy struck her. She fell back. The attempt was stillborn.

The telephone bell kept ringing.

"Answer it, Clara," Kennedy said. "And keep them covered."

He went across the room, opened a drawer in a walnut writing table, and took out some coils of cords. He took these across to Mark, who was doubled up on the floor, all the color drained from his face except for a greenish tinge. He clenched his teeth against the pain, and his lips were curled back. Kennedy tied his wrist together, then his hands behind him.

Clara was saying, "Yes, dear—yes, dear."

Kennedy tied Eve's hands, while Clara kept repeating the words, and covered her with a gun.

"Yes, dear, of course," said Clara. "Don't be long."

She put down the receiver.

"Peter's on his way, Jake. West and the others were at the Guildford cottage, they'll know everything, now. We ought to have got those things away from the cottage before, but I suppose it wouldn't have made much difference in the long run. Peter will soon be here, he's only half an hour away. He'll want to be in at the kill, won't he?"

Eve said, "If you do anything else you'll only make it worse for yourself, for Peter, for—"

"We can't make it worse for Charles, can we?" Clara asked venomously. "And we can't really make it worse for Jake. Nothing's worse than blindness. We all knew the risk, we took it, and we've made West and Lessing suffer. We'll do more, yet. Jake, I think you'd better come to the telephone, and speak to Scotland Yard. If you ask West to come and see you as soon as possible, say you've made a terrible discovery, he'll come. He will always come if he thinks he's going to score a triumph single-handed, that's his weakness. Don't we know it! He'll come. And as he comes in, we'll burn his eyes—"

"Will we, Clara?" Kennedy spoke almost casually. "Yes, I think we can damage his eyes without killing him. I don't want them dead—just blind. I'll die cheerfully, if I know they can't see."

Eve choked, "It's inhuman, it—"

251

Clara strode across the room and struck her over the mouth.

Mark, still on the floor, heard every word.

Roger's car drew up at the corner of Deverall Street, and as he jumped out, Sloan appeared. Two or three other Yard men were hiding in nearby doorways, out of sight. Wilson followed Roger out of the car, Peel came to join the party from the doorway opposite, and they went together in a larger one, out of sight from anyone passing.

"Peter Kennedy here?" asked Roger.

"No. The only thing to report is a message relayed from the Yard. Jacob Kennedy rang up, to ask if you'd come along here. He said he's made a shocking discovery, and that Mark's been hurt. Don't go alone, Roger."

Roger grinned tautly.

"We'll see. I can guess what his shocking discovery is. Peter's told them that we've been to Guildford. They may know about Charles, too. I wouldn't give a snap of the fingers for Mark's life if we're not careful. I know what it's all about, now."

Sloan said, "Sure?"

"Yes. Kennedy's going blind. He's been studying Braille. I found a report by a New York eye specialist, the best man in the world. It's turned Kennedy's brain—and that's probably affected all the family. We don't need any more telling."

Sloan said, "No, I—look! There's Peter."

252

25

The Family

The Yard men watched Peter walk swiftly along the street, on the opposite side to Deverall Court. Obviously he expected the police to be watching, and seemed surprised when none of them appeared. He crossed the road as he reached the flats, without knowing that he had passed four waiting detectives on the way.

He slipped into the main entrance.

Roger went swiftly down the street, reached the entrance a few seconds after the big man, and hurried across to the lift, calling:

"Kennedy! Kennedy, just a minute."

He heard the lift come to a stop, called again, and hurried up the stairs. His right hand was in his pocket as he neared the top. He didn't need his gun then, for Peter appeared, towering above him two steps higher; and he looked savage, ready to do murder.

"What the hell do you want?"

"What's the matter here? Why did your father send for me?"

"Send for you? Did he?" Peter looked surprised, and backed away. "I don't know. I've only just come in."

"Lessing and Mrs. Wedlake are with them. Any idea why?"

Peter grinned. "I couldn't imagine! We'd better go and see."

He swung round and led the way toward the entrance to the flat. He strode along, outpacing Roger, and dug his hand into his pocket for his key. Then he hesitated; there would never be much subtlety in Peter Kennedy.

"Maybe you'd better ring," he said.

"Think so?" Roger grinned—and hit him, a body blow with all his strength behind it. He caught Peter in his tender stomach, the man doubled up and the pain was so great that he didn't even groan. As he fell, Roger grabbed his arm and lowered him quietly. While Peter was still bending forward, Roger slid his hand into the right-hand pocket, and drew out the bunch of keys. There were several Yales, he couldn't be sure which fitted this door. He tried one, very gently; it wouldn't turn the lock.

Peter began to gasp.

Roger tried the second key, and the lock turned. He swung round on Peter, whose lips were parted and who was groaning now. As he did so, Sloan and Peel appeared at the head of the stairs. They came up swiftly and silently, and dragged Peter away, still groaning.

Roger turned the key in the lock again, and pushed the door wider open. He heard Clara speak, but didn't catch the words. He pushed the door wide enough for him to step through. Several other doors in the flat were open, and light streamed from each. He heard Clara again, and the sound of her voice came from a room almost immediately opposite the front door. He stepped into the hall, while Sloan and Peel waited outside the open front door; others were looking after Peter.

Clara said, "Peter ought to be here soon."

"Don't forget that the police are probably outside, and might hold him up," said Kennedy. "That doesn't matter, all we want is West. Once he steps in here, we'll have him." He laughed on a high-pitched note—then stopped. "Then we'll do you, Lessing."

There was silence, followed by a sharp hiss. A woman cried out, and it wouldn't be Clara. Roger stepped to the side of the hall, crept along close to the door, until he could see one corner of the room, a chair, and Eve sitting in it; she was bound hand and foot.

He couldn't see Mark.

Clara said hoarsely, "Do Lessing first. And you ought to do the girl, she —"

"No, I couldn't blind our Eve," said Kennedy. "She had a good reason for what she did, we're the last to complain about anyone acting through a sense of family loyalty, aren't we? That's the one way we've been lucky, Clara. With the boys. We've trained them well, we've identical interests, no one could have been more loyal."

"And—Charles is dead," Clara said in a taut voice.

"We'll soon follow him," said Kennedy. "Didn't we agree that rather than be caught we would kill ourselves? We won't give West the satisfaction of catching us and putting us on trial. Just a dose of this, one for him and one for Lessing, and then—get the tablets out of your bag, Clara. Don't let's have any regrets. The one thing I hope is that Peter gets back before West comes."

"West won't come." That was Mark, in a muted voice. "He won't be fool enough to come."

"You don't know West as well as you think you do," said Kennedy softly. "He fancies he's so good, and he always takes chances on his own. Especially when he knows there's danger. It's a kind of mock heroics. He likes to hit the headlines and to be called a hero, so he pretends he does it to save others from being hurt. Instead, it's just to feed his vanity. He won't have much more vanity left when—"

The hissing sound came again; and Roger saw the tip of a tongue of flame.

He didn't need more telling what Kennedy was planning; the man was holding a kind of flame-thrower. Roger couldn't guess its range; it probably didn't matter. He could make sure that it wasn't turned on him, but couldn't be sure that it wouldn't be turned onto Mark or the girl. He had just one chance of assuring that.

He was close to the edge of the door.

"Get the tablets," Kennedy repeated. "Cyanide is very quick, my dear. They're in the bedroom, aren't they? We owe them to Doc Gorley. Poor Doc. He—"

Clara turned toward the door, her bustling movements unmistakable, even now. Roger flattened himself against the wall, as she appeared. She came right into the hall before she saw that the front door was ajar.

She screamed.

256

Roger darted forward, saw Kennedy standing near Mark, saw the gun with the long snout in his hand. Roger fired at the hand holding the gun. He fired again, as Kennedy tried to turn and as his finger pressed the trigger, involuntarily. A tongue of flame spat out and hit the carpet. The pile caught, and the stench of burning and of smoke leaped into the room.

Clara screamed again.

Sloan and Peel grabbed her before she could reach the room.

Next morning, just before twelve o'clock, Roger went into Chatworth's office, and the Assistant Commissioner actually stood up, to stretch out an arm and shake hands. He was smiling, and looked almost smug as he pushed cigarettes toward Roger, and then waved to a chair.

"Sit down, Roger. Tell me all about it. Remind me, too, that if you really have to get a move on, you ought to be angry."

His beam was almost ludicrous.

Roger, primed with the full report, sat down and watched the A.C., with his head on one side.

He said, "What's that?"

"You heard. When you're really mad, you get quicker results than when you're cool and dispassionate. One of the things that even I have noticed about you."

"Well, well," breathed Roger. "So you slanged Mark Lessing because you thought it would make me mad."

"That's right."

Roger grinned. "Well, it didn't—I swallowed that bait of squeezing Mark out, hook, line, and

257

sinker. If they hadn't killed our dog, and shown me that if they really set out to get me or the boys they could, I—"

"I know, I know," said Chatworth. "How are they all?"

"Fine."

"Good. Now, I've seen the first reports. Tell me what I don't already know, will you?"

Roger leaned back in his chair.

"You probably know most of it, by now. That Kennedy blamed us for the fact that he was going blind. He had always blamed me for sending him down, and it was easy for him to blame me for this too. He began the plot as soon as the New York specialist told him that his sight could have been saved if he could have gone to him while in prison.

"What we didn't realize was that the family was behind him. They were all in it together, and covered their traces brilliantly. As soon as Kennedy found Mark was interested in him he knew he was under suspicion, so he tried to make himself look like a victim of the same man who was after me. Hence the blackmail business, the appeal for police help, the attack on him in the car—all put up for our benefit. Eve helped him more than she knew, because she'd worked for Wiseman, and confused the trails. Kennedy and Peter had used her typewriter at the beginning, and kept on using it to make us suspect her. For the same reason they had Doc Gorley murdered in her flat. She was right about Kennedy and Wiseman once working together, but Wiseman wasn't mixed up in this."

"Sure?"

"Quite sure. Eve told us part of the truth, about wanting to avenge her husband, but another reason she had for working with Kennedy was to find out what was happening to her sister-in-law. Wasted effort, but—I think it's a good thing she tried to do it. She didn't tell us that, didn't say anything about the cottage and the dog until the last minute. Actually she made up the story of seeing Charles and Mavis in the car and then pumping Peter, to prevent us from asking her why she hadn't told us before. She knew that her sister-in-law was involved with Charles Kennedy, but didn't want to drag her in. She felt she couldn't hold out any longer, after Mark told her everything that had happened. She knew then that it was Mavis who had set the dog on Richard and was sure Charles was involved. So she told Mark about the Horsham cottage and started us on the final stage."

"Nice girl," said Chatworth.

"They don't come any better." Roger changed the subject. "I thought I'd check everything that could be checked about Kennedy and all the suspects, but missed one thing—their prison records. If I'd studied them I'd have seen that Kennedy complained about eye pain, and was examined by several specialists. They all said it was too late to save his eyes, that an operation would be useless. Kennedy would go blind, if he had long enough to live. He came out of jail, actually tried to resign himself and started to learn Braille—and then was recommended to the New York specialist. When he was told his sight could have been saved he was obsessed by one thought: revenge.

"He didn't want to kill me or Mark. He wanted to blind us both, to cause us as much suffering as possible, to make us know pain and fear. That was why he had Mark's books torn up, and then Mark

259

attacked with ammonia. That was why he had the school milk poisoned, and my boys scared at Bournemouth, and why Snicker was killed.

"They used everyone they could. Mavis Hill was in love with Charles, and Charles turned her bad. When Eve took an interest, Mavis fitted into the family plans nicely. It's the first case of a vendetta against the Yard I've come across."

"Against the Yard!"

Roger smiled faintly.

"Won't that do, sir? There was also a secret store of money Jacob Kennedy had managed to put away before we caught him, he had a useful cache in a dozen different countries. When he'd satisfied himself about Mark and me, he would have left England, of course. Now—"

"The men will hang," said Chatworth abruptly. "Clara will get fifteen years at least."

A month after the hanging of Jacob and Peter Kennedy and of Benson, Mark Lessing and Eve Wedlake got out of Mark's car, outside the Bell Street house. Janet, who was expecting them for the evening, was at the bedroom window. She waved and disappeared, and was at the front door before they reached it. Roger was just behind her, and from an unseen corner came a muffled giggling.

"It's not yet seven," Mark said. "Having a half-day's holiday, Roger?"

"Keep that up, and you'll become an Assistant Commissioner one of these days," said Roger. He shook hands; and held Eve's tightly. "Nice to see you again, Eve. How are you?"

"I couldn't be happier," she told him.

He glanced at her left hand; she'd already taken the glove off. The engagement ring shone and sparkled, a superb solitaire.

Janet kissed her.

"When?" she asked.

"Soon," said Mark. "Registry Office and no fuss, but we want to make sure it's a day when you and Roger can come. Not to mention the infants. Where are they, by the way?"

The giggling reached a climax—and suddenly two figures leaped into sight on the landing and came racing down the stairs. Behind them a little fluffy bundle almost fell, yapping excitedly. Scoopy flung himself at Mark, Richard at Eve, and the fluffy bundle hurled himself about in all directions.

Mark caught Janet's eye.

"Quite over it?" he asked.

"They were still edgy about dogs, so we thought we'd try this."

"Isn't he *won*derful?" cried Scoopy. "The front part's mine and the back part's Richard's, so he's *ours*."

By the year 2000, 2 out of 3 Americans could be illiterate.

It's true.

Today, 75 million adults...about one American in three, can't read adequately. And by the year 2000, U.S. News & World Report envisions an America with a literacy rate of only 30%.

Before that America comes to be, you can stop it...by joining the fight against illiteracy today.

Call the Coalition for Literacy at toll-free **1-800-228-8813** and volunteer.

**Volunteer
Against Illiteracy.
The only degree you need
is a degree of caring.**

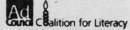

Ad Council Coalition for Literacy